"Mom, Dad, I have to talk to you. I—I didn't have the flu."

"I suspected you weren't really sick," Mom said. "It's all right. We understand."

"No, you don't. There's something wrong with me—really wrong. We lost the tournament because I couldn't use my right arm. Sometimes my neck hurts, and sometimes my knee or elbow hurts. And sometimes my knee and elbow get swollen." Tears welled up in my eyes. "Oh, Mom, what's wrong with me?"

Never Look Back

Alida Young

To my father, Albert Johnson; to his sisters, Lottie, Frieda, and Nellie; and to my cousin Eleanor, who is like a sister to me.

Special thanks to Andrea Kovalesky, R.N., M.S.N. at Childrens Hospital of Los Angeles; Bebe Green, Director of the Arthritis Foundation, Coachella Valley Branch; Joel Hirschberg, M.D. Rheumatology; Steen E. Mortensen, M.D. Rheumatology at Loma Linda Medical Center; Rob Rennebohm, M.D. Rheumatology; Lynn Colby, M.S., P.T.; Linda L. Wetherbee, Vice President for the American Juvenile Arthritis Organization and Special Groups; John Weeks, staff writer for *The Sun*; Kevin Smit; Colleen Blair; Cammy and Linda Holbrook.

Cover photo by Gene Woolridge

Published by Willowisp Press, Inc.
401 E. Wilson Bridge Road, Worthington, Ohio 43085

Copyright ©1987 by Willowisp Press, Inc.

Printed in the United States of America
10 9 8 7 6 5 4 3 2

ISBN 0-87406-286-1

One

"COME on, Heather! Strike! Get another strike!"

I had already bowled six strikes in a row. I rubbed my fingers above the hand dryer, picked up my bowling ball, and rolled it around in my hands for a second. I glanced back at my teammates who were standing behind me, holding their breath. There wasn't a sound in the place as I stepped up to take my last shot. I swallowed hard, made my approach, and sent the ball down the alley. I closed my eyes and breathed the words "Strike . . . strike . . ."

A yell went up, and I opened my eyes to see all ten pins go down. Everybody in the place was clapping. My four teammates—Denise, April, Jill, and Ginny—rushed up and hugged me.

"If you bowl like that in the tournament, we're going to beat the Ridgefield team so badly that they'll take up tiddlywinks," Denise said, giving me the biggest hug of all.

The five of us (we call ourselves the Stars) all started talking at once. We got something from the soft-drink machine and headed to our favorite booth in the corner.

Doug Warren came over and leaned his long, lanky body against a post. Ever since his dad died three years ago, he and his mother have run the bowling alley. It's not like some alleys I've been in. There are ping-pong tables and a video arcade. Mrs. Warren doesn't let anyone smoke here, and she sets aside time just for kids. The place is so popular that it attracts people from as far away as Ridgefield, Port Andrews, and Neptune Beach.

"Great game, Heather," Doug said to me. But all the time he was staring at April.

Boys always stare at her. She has blond hair and big, blue eyes.

I sighed, wishing boys would look at me the way they look at April—especially Doug. I've liked him since first grade. I still have the present he gave me for my seventh birthday. It's an agate with markings like a star. He found it on the beach. The agate gave me the idea to call our group the Stars.

"Thanks," I said to Doug, when he finally turned his attention to me. "That's the very first time I ever bowled over 200."

"Well, you had a good teacher," he said,

patting himself on the back. "If you Stars beat the Ridgefield Rockets, I think my mother will sponsor you. She might even spring for uniforms."

"Hey, that's great," April said. "I want pink shirts."

April is a lot more interested in the uniforms than in bowling. Her favorite exercise is turning the knob on the TV to watch a soap opera.

"Douglas," Mrs. Warren called. "I need you at the cash register."

Doug grinned. "Money calls. See you later."

"I think he's the cutest guy in town," Ginny whispered. "You'd never guess he's so muscular until you see him without a shirt."

Denise giggled. "So when did you see him without his shirt?"

"At the beach, of course," Ginny said, but she turned pink.

"Well, in Rocky Cove he doesn't have much competition," April said. "I hate this crummy little town. No guys, no movies, no decent shops, and—no guys. I can't wait until we go to high school. My sister says Ridgefield is full of good-looking guys."

Ridgefield's about 12 miles away. It's not a whole lot bigger than Rocky Cove, but at least they have a high school. And you can go to a movie or a skating rink. Rocky Cove isn't a tourist town, so there aren't many businesses and souvenir shops. But my dad says it's the best town in Oregon.

The Stars spend a lot of time talking about guys. We do other things together, too. But then we pair off, and one person is always left out. It's weird how it works. We never really plan it, but we all take our turn being the "fifth wheel." I really hate it when I'm that person. My grandpa says that when it's my turn I'm as cranky as a bear with a sore nose.

As I sipped my drink, I looked at the other four. They were arguing about whether or not Doug would ask April for a date.

I don't know which Star I like best. April is the prettiest. Ginny is the smartest. We all go to her when we need help with our homework. Jill will probably be the most successful one. Just about everybody in her family is a doctor. Well, actually her dad's a veterinarian. She wants to be a surgeon. Denise is really the nicest of the Stars. She'll do anything for you—sometimes more than you want.

Me—I can't figure out. I'm not the prettiest (I have plain old brownish blond hair) or the smartest (I get *B*'s) or the nicest. (I have a dimple in my chin, and my grandpa says, "Dimple in the chin—devil within.") And I'll never be a doctor. (I mean, I get queasy if someone picks a scab!) I'm going to be a long-distance runner, and my dream is to be in the Olympics. Doug and I are both training for the third annual Rocky Cove 10-kilometer run. It's on October eighteenth, just two weeks away. Last year I came in second in my age group.

"Hey, Heather, what do you think?" Jill asked.

"What . . . ?" I hadn't heard half of what they'd said.

"Do you think I should invite anybody else to my party?" April wanted to know.

Jill laughed. "I told her—only if she invites boys."

"If I invite Chrissy Aldrich," April said, "we'd be an even number."

Ginny groaned. "Yeah, but who'd want to be stuck with her? She's too depressing. All she talks about is her asthma and her dumb allergies."

"I feel sorry for her," Denise said. "She always looks like she's cry—" She stopped in midsentence to look at me. "Heather, what's wrong?"

I stared at her in surprise. "Wrong?"

"Does your arm hurt?"

I looked down, realizing I was unconsciously rubbing my elbow. "Guess I must have hit my crazy bone or something. It's nothing."

April glanced at her watch. "Ginny, we have to go if I'm going to trim your hair.

April's almost as good as a regular hairdresser. She wants to go to modeling school, and says models have to be able to do their own hair and makeup.

As we all got up to leave, I spoke to Denise. "Want to run for a while?" Denise isn't really into cross-country running, but she had helped me train the last two weeks.

"I'm sorry," Denise said. "I promised Jill I'd help her with her science project."

"Oh . . . sure . . . ."

Nuts! It was my turn to be the fifth wheel.

* * * * *

The market my parents own is next door to the bowling alley. It's just like all the other weathered buildings that hug the coast highway.

My Grandpa Al Quick built and ran the grocery and meat market. When he retired, my mom and dad took over and modernized the place. Our name is Ames, but the store is still called Quick's Quality Market.

We live in an apartment over the store. Sometimes I hate the market, because Mom and Dad are always so busy. Mom does all the ordering, waits on customers, and keeps the books. Dad waits on customers, too, and does everything else.

I went in through the market to tell Mom I was going running.

I waited while she finished making change for Mrs. Jensen. Mom is getting so big now that she has trouble bending over. Can you believe it? She's pregnant! She's 40, and she's going to have a baby! My parents had been married for five years before they had me. Now, 13 years later, they're having another baby. By the time the kid's my age, they'll be old. I mean, can you imagine them going to PTA and stuff?

Mrs. Jensen smiled at me as she was leaving. "Well, Heather, aren't you excited? Just think, you'll have a little brother or sister to play with."

I forced a smile. "Oh, yes—excited." *I'll probably have to baby-sit all the time*, I thought. My bedroom has already been made into a nursery so the baby will be as close as possible to Mom and Dad's room. I have to sleep on the sofa bed in Dad's tiny office off the living room.

Dad called from the meat block where he was cutting steaks. "Heather, there's a sack of crabs upstairs. They're for a special order, and I'd like you to cook them."

I hate the idea of cooking crabs alive. And I'm scared one is going to take my finger off someday.

11

"There are enough for our dinner, too," Mom said. "Put them all in to chill when you're finished. And ask your grandfather to join us tonight. I haven't been able to get him on the phone, and you know how he loves crab."

Grandpa Al is Mom's dad. He lives above the bowling alley. He can't hear very well, so he doesn't mind the racket from the bowling alley. And he gets cheap rent.

I got out of there fast before Mom and Dad thought of something else for me to do. Saturday afternoons were supposed to be all my own.

I went through to the back of the store and up the inside stairs that lead to our apartment. Usually, I take the steps two at a time, but today I was worn out—from all the excitement of bowling over 200, I guess.

I put my bowling bag in the hall closet and headed for the kitchen. Then I put a huge pot of water on the stove to boil.

While the crabs were cooking and stinking up the whole place, I tried to call Grandpa from the wall phone in the kitchen. There was no answer. I hurried down the stairs, crossed a narrow field, and climbed up the long staircase to his apartment. I knocked, then opened the door and yelled, "Grandpa Al!"

He was in his big chair in front of the TV.

His apartment is full of things he's collected over the years. He has hundreds of shells and agates and weirdly shaped pieces of driftwood from the beach. He even has a couple of large glass balls the size of beach balls that had washed up on the beach years ago. He says Japanese fishermen used them as floats for their nets.

I crossed to the chair, poked him on the shoulder, and shouted, "Grandpa Al!"

He jumped a foot and glared at me. He's a big, strong man, and he has a deep line between his eyes that makes him look really mean. His voice is gruff, and some of the kids are scared of him. But he's not mean at all, and I love him a lot. I hugged him. "Hi, Grandpa Al. Sorry I startled you. Mom says to come to dinner. We're having crab. I'm cooking them now."

He tweaked my nose the way he's been doing since I was little. "Then what are you doing up here, girl? Never overcook a crab."

I rubbed my nose. It hurts when he tweaks it. "You didn't answer the phone."

"It didn't ring," he growled.

He won't wear a hearing aid and won't even admit he's going deaf. He reads lips pretty well, but if his back is turned—forget it.

"I guess I dialed wrong," I said. "See you at seven."

"I'll bring the checkerboard. We can get in a game after dinner."

"Sure," I told him, although I was getting kind of tired of checkers.

I used to spend a lot of time with Grandpa. He taught me how to play checkers, pop popcorn in a fireplace, ride my bike, and do about a hundred other things. But since his hearing has gotten so bad, it's not as much fun to be with him. My throat gets sore from yelling.

I kissed him on the top of his nearly bald head, yanked his beard, and got out of his reach before he could tweak my nose again. "See you at dinner," I shouted.

On the way downstairs, I was surprised to see Doug headed toward the beach in his sweats. Usually he trains in the morning before school.

"Hi, Heather. Are you going running?"

Actually, I'd just about decided not to go. With all the running up and down stairs and cooking crabs, I was beat. "Sure," I said quickly. "I just have to put the crabs in to chill and tell Mom where I'm going."

Tired or not, I wasn't going to miss a chance to run with Doug—even if he did beat me all the time.

* * * * *

"You aren't moving as smoothly as you usually do," Doug shouted over the sound of the surf. "Got a blister?"

We'd been running for a couple of miles, keeping to the damp sand at the edge of the water, and dodging waves and piles of seaweed.

"I'm just a little tired today," I said.

"Want to stop?"

"No!" I wasn't going to let him think I was a baby. "Let's go down to the dunes and run in the deep sand for a while. It'll strengthen our legs."

He looked at me doubtfully. "Are you sure you want to?"

"Of course I'm sure. I'm just getting my second wind." And to prove it, I put on a burst of speed and passed him. I turned and yelled back over my shoulder, "You can't catch me!"

"Watch out for that sea—"

My foot hit a big hunk of slippery seaweed, and I went sprawling. If I'd been a bowling ball I'd have made a strike. My right knee hit a rock or a piece of driftwood—something hard. For a second, a wave of nausea swept over me, and I thought I was going to throw up.

Doug knelt down beside me. "Heather! Are you okay?" He didn't try to move me. "Where do you hurt?"

Moving slowly, I sat up. "Just my dumb

knee, I think." I blew out my breath. "It's nothing." I gritted my teeth and got to my feet. "But I don't think I want to run on the dunes."

As we walked slowly home, I figured my knee would start feeling better. But it didn't. It hurt—really hurt.

If I've ruined my chances to win the 10K run, I thought, *I'm going to bury myself in the sand and cover myself with seaweed and crabs.*

Two

EARLY on the Sunday of the Rocky Cove run, the morning was crisp and bright and perfect. The ocean was glassy smooth and shiny like blue-gray ice. Doug and I ate our prerun breakfast at Margie's Diner. It's a tiny place with just a counter and three booths and crazy signs like WE DON'T SERVE CRABS and CHILI TODAY; HOT TAMALE. Doug and I ordered a high-carbohydrate breakfast of buttermilk pancakes and fruit.

While we waited for our order, Doug looked at me and frowned. "Are you sure you ought to run today?"

"Why not?" I asked sharply.

"Ever since you fell a couple of weeks ago, I haven't seen you training."

I avoided his eyes. "I haven't exactly been lying around."

But he was right. I hadn't trained the way I should have. You'd think after nearly two weeks that my knee would have gotten better.

17

But it still hurt. I hadn't told anyone, especially my mom. She never had liked the idea of my running. She'd heard somewhere that girls who run a lot get eating disorders from trying to keep their weight down. *That won't ever happen to me,* I thought. Although lately, I haven't had much of an appetite.

Margie set the pancakes in front of me. They looked wonderful, but I could only eat a little. I probably just had a case of prerace nerves.

When we finished, we headed down to Rocky Cove Park at the edge of town. I could see the population sign. It said 1,637. I wondered if it would change to 1,638 when my mother had her baby.

It was several hours until race time, but already I could feel the excitement in the park. The run was to start at 10:00. It was timed to hit low tide. The officials' stand was set up, and a mobile unit from radio station KROC was playing rock music over a loudspeaker. A lot of out-of-towners had arrived the night before in motor homes, vans, and pickups.

We joined a group of people by the picnic area. Runners always have a lot to talk about, and today they were all excited because Tim Hunter and BeBe Johnson were going to be here. They're big names in the running world.

I was worried about my knee. It hurt like a

toothache, and I couldn't seem to get my mind off it. Several runners were complaining about their injuries. I figured they were making excuses, in case they didn't do well. No matter how badly my knee hurt, I wasn't going to talk about it.

Whenever I sat too long, my knee got stiff, so I headed over to pay my late-entry fee and get my run number. I'd waited to be sure my knee was well enough. Mrs. Marsh, the mayor's wife, was taking the entries.

My number was 8097. "I hope there aren't that many people entered." I laughed.

"No," Mrs. Marsh said, "but we have many more people than we expected." She smiled. "Good luck, Heather."

I nodded my thanks. The way my leg felt, I was going to need plenty of luck.

"Have you seen the other Stars?" I asked as I pinned my number on the front of my shirt.

"They're already at the aid station getting drinks and sponges ready." The four of them had volunteered for the job.

I was wearing my sweats over my blue shorts and T-shirt, but I still felt chilled. To keep warm, I walked around for a bit. Then I sat for a while, but I was too nervous to sit for long. The butterflies were already fluttering in my stomach, and I wished I hadn't eaten any of those pancakes.

I used up most of my time standing in line for the restrooms—two different times. Once the run starts, you're out of luck. Last year, I nearly died because I forgot to go just before the race started.

When it got close to 10:00, I warmed up. I did my stretching exercises, jogged in place for a few minutes to get my heart pumping, then cooled down again. I took off my sweats and shivered in the wind that had come up. The red and yellow flags and banners were waving briskly.

I headed over to the starting area and passed an ambulance. Last year, two people had needed emergency help—one with heat exhaustion and one with a sprained ankle.

Ten kilometers is a little over six miles. My average in a 10K run is 50 minutes, but my best time was last year—46:32. I got in line according to my time, which put me fairly near the front. I said hi to Gretchen Lundquist. She had taken first place in our age group last year. I was second, only 10 seconds behind her. Doug was just in front of us, along with the fastest runners in the older age groups.

I felt sorry for the slower runners. They were so far back, they had to run farther than anybody else. The loudspeaker crackled and sputtered. Then the race official's voice blared out, "Welcome to the Third Annual Rocky

Cove 10K Run."

Everybody yelled and clapped.

The official gave us instructions and some safety tips about pacing ourselves, knowing our limits, and not running too close together.

"The run starts here at the park, goes down to the beach for five kilometers, then up the old highway and back to here. The tide's low, so you'll have hard-packed sand to run on. We have water and sponges if you need them. But the temperature is only 52 degrees right now, so heat won't be a problem like last year."

"Heather!" I heard my name shouted. "Heather, over here!"

I turned to see Mom and Dad waving. Dad put up two fingers in a victory sign. I waved back. I hadn't really expected to see them until the end of the run, but I was glad they were there.

"One minute," the announcer called.

I felt a tap on my shoulder. It was Doug.

"Good luck, Heather."

His words almost echoed the run announcer's. "Good luck, everybody. Don't forget to stick around for the drawing. We have some terrific prizes."

I could already feel my heart pumping faster.

"Thirty seconds . . . ten . . . five . . . two . . . one!"

The starter's gun sounded, triggering the electronic clock and my adrenaline. The horde of runners surged forward. Someone stepped on my heels. Someone else bumped into me, knocking me into the runner to my left. It sounded and felt as if the earth were moving.

At first we were jammed too close to get up any speed, but after a couple of kilometers, the pack spread out. Overhead, a few sea gulls circled and dipped, screeching at me as if encouraging me to run faster.

I saw Doug ahead of me, with only a few older men in front of him. Gretchen was almost even with me.

At the 4K marker, someone shouted the time. I was doing okay.

Then suddenly, a sharp, burning pain hit my knee, and I almost screamed out loud. I pulled up short and stumbled off to the side. Dozens of people passed me without even a look. For a moment, the pain took my breath away, then it eased up a bit. *Come on, Heather,* I thought. *Don't let anyone else pass you.*

I straightened up and took off again. But every time I came down on my right foot, it felt as if someone were stabbing me with a hot knife. I was almost sick from the pain. I kept going, but so slowly now that more and more people were passing me.

The aid station was at the 5K mark. Maybe

a drink of water would help. I yelled, "Water!" April handed me a drink, while Ginny cheered me on. I drank the cool water and tossed the paper cup aside. As I passed the table where Denise and Jill were handling the sponges, I grabbed one and squeezed the water over my head.

Denise started running along beside me. "Heather? You're way behind your time. Are you okay?"

"Just a cramp," I yelled, and tried to pick up speed to prove to her that I was okay.

But at the turn away from the beach and up the hill to the highway, I had to slow down to almost a walk. Tears of pain and frustration welled up in my eyes, and I could hardly see. At the 7K mark at the top of the hill, my knee just gave way, and I fell in a heap.

A man passed me and called, "I'll send help back."

In moments the ambulance was there. "I don't need you guys. It's just a cramp," I lied. "I'll be fine."

"Get in, and we'll take you back to the park," the medical technician said.

I was so far behind now that it didn't make that much difference. One of the medics helped me into the ambulance. At the edge of the park, I asked them to let me out. I didn't want to face anybody yet. I sat half-hidden on a bench by a stunted cedar tree.

All the serious runners had finished. The last of the slow ones were struggling in now. The Ridgefield High band was playing between drawings for prizes. The drawings were a way to keep the crowd around until the awards ceremony.

The runners' names and times were posted on a large board. From this distance I couldn't see the board well enough to know how Doug had done. He and some other kids were eating the yogurt, fruit, and soft drinks that had been donated for the runners.

"And for a pair of running shoes from Sports Unlimited in Ridgefield—the number is 8097," the loudspeaker blared. For a second I didn't realize it was my number. I sat where I was. I didn't deserve to win any kind of prize.

I saw my parents at the roped-off area at the finish line. I knew they must be worried about me. I had to face them sometime. Getting slowly to my feet, I hobbled over to them. I couldn't pretend to them that I had a leg cramp. After this, Mom would never let me run again.

* * * * *

"Mom, I don't want to go to the doctor," I said, and got up slowly from the dinner table.

"I only have a sore knee."

"Don't argue, Heather. I saw you wince just then when you got up from the chair. And it's not the first time. I'm taking you to see the doctor tomorrow. I knew you shouldn't have been running."

Dad helped himself to more salad. "Don't baby her, Sheila. When I used to run, I'd get shinsplints and sore knees. You can't go see a doctor every time you have a little pain."

"Daddy's right," I said. "I fell. I could have hurt myself just as easily by falling down the stairs. Please, Mom, I don't want to see Dr. Cornwell."

"Old quack," Grandpa Al muttered. "I wouldn't send my pet turtle to him."

Grandpa Al thinks all doctors are quacks. That's one reason why he won't wear a hearing aid.

"He's the only doctor in town," Mom said. "At least he can tell you what to do about it. I have my checkup with him tomorrow afternoon. Maybe he can fit you in then."

I knew there was no point in saying anything more. Mom is stubborn. Grandpa Al says Mom and I take after him when it comes to being bullheaded.

So instead of going to bowling practice the next day, I had to see old Cornball. That's what the kids call him.

He has a musty old office near the park. Inside, it smells like medicine and pine cleaner. There's a window that's covered with a piece of wood. Every year the wind blows out windows all over town.

"The doctor will see you now, Mrs. Ames," the nurse said.

I leafed through some old magazines until the nurse called for me. I followed her to the examining room.

Doctor Cornwell is even older than Grandpa Al. He looks kind of like a skinny walrus. He's usually out fishing, but he doesn't look strong enough to pull in a sardine. He had me sit on a paper-covered table. "Well, well, so we did something to our leg, did we?" he asked.

I rolled up the leg of my cords. "It's my right knee. A while back I fell. It still hurts."

"Open wide," he said, and placed a stick on my tongue. "How old are you, young lady?"

"Glug . . . thir . . . glug . . . teen." How did he expect me to talk with the stick down my throat?

Then he listened to my chest and tapped my back.

"It's my knee that hurts," I mumbled.

Mom shook her head to shush me.

The doctor took my blood pressure and pulse. Finally, he got around to my knee, poking and prodding and making me lift my leg.

"It appears to be a strain from the fall," he said. "It'll just take time. Take a couple of aspirin, put cold packs on it, and stay off the leg."

And then—you won't believe this—he gave me a sucker and a balloon from a dusty box on the desk! When he delivers Mom's baby, he'll probably smack it on the bottom and hand it a balloon and a sucker.

I was relieved that my knee was only strained. I'd been worrying that maybe I'd damaged it seriously so I couldn't run for a long time. I'd just about die if I couldn't run.

* * * * *

I did everything the doctor had told me to do. I didn't run, I didn't bowl, and I had my knee in so much ice, I thought I'd get frostbite.

But by Halloween the knee wasn't any better, so I decided I wasn't going to stay off my leg any longer. That night, April's dad was taking the Stars skating in Ridgefield. Afterward, everybody was going to stay overnight at April's. I was going to go—doctor or no doctor. But I still had to deal with Mom and Dad.

Sunday was the only day we all ate together. Other evenings, either Dad or Mom had to be downstairs in the market. I waited until we were ready for dessert. I'd baked Dad's

27

favorite brownies, the extra-chocolaty kind.

"Mom? Dad? May I go with the Stars to Ridgefield tonight? April's dad is taking us."

"Where?" Dad asked. "To a party or a movie?"

"Skating," I mumbled.

"Howard," Mom said softly, and got up from the table.

"Heather, you've been hobbling around here for days," Dad said. "And now you want to go skating!"

"Howard," Mom said again. "I think we're going to have to get ready to go to the hospital."

Dad jumped up so fast that he knocked over his chair. "Sheila, just take it easy. Heather, get her bag and coat. And bring a blanket. I'll go warm up the truck."

I stood there frozen for a minute.

"Heather, honey, it's all right," Mom said calmly. "My bag's all packed. My blue coat and the blanket are on the foot of my bed."

I ran to her and hugged her. "Mom, are you okay? Will you get to the hospital in time?" The closest one was 30 miles away.

"Of course I will. There should be plenty of time."

While I got her things, she tried to call Grandpa Al. As usual, he didn't answer the phone.

Dad and I helped Mom down the stairs. "You go stay with Grandpa," Mom said to me. "Tell him we'll let him know as soon as he has a new grandchild."

I waited until the pickup was out of sight, then called April to tell her I couldn't go with them. I got my pajamas and toothbrush and the candy for the trick-or-treaters. As I headed for Grandpa's apartment, it was just starting to get dark. The little kids would be out soon.

I hadn't climbed Grandpa's steep stairs for a week or so, and it really hurt. I guess it was a good thing I wasn't going skating.

Grandpa was watching the news. But I had bigger news than what was on TV. "Grandpa Al!" I shouted. "Mom just left for the hospital. They'll phone as soon as the baby's born." I flung my arms around him. "Grandpa, I'm scared."

He pulled me onto his lap the way he used to do when I was little, and rocked back and forth. "Your mother's strong and healthy. She comes from good stock."

"But she's not young anymore."

"Humfph," he said. "My mama had her sixth baby when she was 44. And she did it practically all by herself."

Grandpa went on, telling me about his mom. He made having a baby sound easy and natural. I started feeling a little better about it.

"Let's play a game of checkers," Grandpa said. "Set up the board."

Sometimes I beat him, but tonight I couldn't seem to keep my mind on the game. I kept thinking about Mom. It took me forever to make a move.

"Are you going to play or sit there like a toad?" he asked impatiently.

The doorbell rang. I jumped up and nearly yelled from the pain in my knee. I limped to the door. Five little kids in scary masks held out sacks and yelled, "Trick or treat!"

I pretended to be scared, and gave each one of them a bunch of goodies. When I sat back down again, Grandpa grumbled, "A stupid holiday. Probably started by a dentist," he said as he helped himself to a candy bar.

Before I could make another move, the bell rang again . . . and again. We get every kid in town, because we give candy bars from the store. I felt like a bouncing ball. And all the getting up and down was making my knee really hurt.

The bell rang again. Grandpa didn't hear it, but when I got up again, he slapped a checker on the board with a bang. "Don't answer it. Turn off all the lights, and we'll pretend we're not home."

I sighed and got up slowly, lifting myself with my arms. "They already know we're here." I got a handful of candy and opened the door.

"Trick or treat," Doug said with a grin.

"Aren't you a little old for this?" I asked, trying not to let him know I was glad to see him. I hadn't seen much of him since the run. He'd won first place in his age group and fourth in the overall.

"I just came up to find out about your mom," he said. "We saw her and your dad take off with a suitcase."

"Come on in, son," Grandpa said. "And take off that silly mask."

Doug grinned. He was used to Grandpa. "Hi, Grandpa Al," he said. "Do you have a new grandbaby yet?"

"Mom and Dad only left for the hospital a couple of hours ago," I said.

Doug was still standing near the door. "Well, I guess I'd better go. I don't want to interrupt your game. I—uh—Mom and I just wanted to see if everything was okay."

"Come set your bones for a spell," Grandpa Al said. "This checker game is a disaster." He looked at me, then at Doug. "I'll make some popcorn. We can turn off the lights, and I'll tell you some ghost stories. How about it?"

"It sounds good to me," Doug said, then added quickly, "if it's okay with Heather."

Without waiting for my answer, Grandpa

headed for the kitchen. I gave an offhand shrug, but secretly I could have hugged Grandpa for inviting Doug to stay. I wouldn't even mind hearing Grandpa's stories for the hundredth time.

As I sat down, my knee seemed to collapse, and I practically fell into the chair. Doug rushed over to me. "Heather! Are you okay?"

"Sure." I tried to keep the fear out of my voice. "I just lost my balance."

"Just like you had a cramp in your leg at the run? You can't kid me, Heather. You're in a lot of pain."

Tears sprang to my eyes. "Doug, please don't tell anybody, but I think there's something terribly wrong. It . . . it seems worse than just a strained knee."

Three

AT 6:00 the next morning, while Grandpa and I were eating breakfast, the phone rang. I hurried to answer it. "Hello?"

"Heather, it's Dad. You have a seven-pound, six-ounce baby brother. He's beautiful."

"Is Mom okay?"

"She's fine, honey. She and the baby will stay here a few days, though. I'll be home by eight. Henry Bigelow will be in to help out for a couple of weeks, but ask your grandpa to open the store for me. Mom sends you two a big hug and a kiss. I have to go. I'll see you in a couple of hours." He hung up before I could ask any questions.

Grandpa was sitting by me. "Well—well, what did Howard say? Is Sheila all right?"

I repeated what Dad had told me. "Do you think Mom is really okay?"

He put his arms around me. "I told you, your mother's strong as an ox." He was beaming. "A grandson. It's about time."

I pulled back, feeling a little hurt. *What was a granddaughter—a bowl of cottage cheese?*

He patted my shoulder. "I'll get on down to the store. Don't know why your dad asked Henry to help out, though. I can handle it."

I watched him get out his white butcher apron and roll up his shirtsleeves. He looked about 10 years younger. I wasn't sure whether it was because he was going back to work or because he had a new grandson.

* * * * *

Mom and Dad named the baby Joseph Alfred Ames, which made Grandpa Al happy. I decided I'd call the baby Joey. The hospital didn't allow 13-year-olds to see patients, so I only got to peek at Joey through a window. All I saw was a tiny, wrinkled face.

Dad brought daily bulletins, mostly about how wonderful little Joseph was. "He looks strong, like a football player," Dad said. To be honest, I got a little tired of hearing about nothing but Joey.

On Wednesday, Dad and Grandpa closed up the market early and came upstairs where I was doing my homework. "I'm going to pick up your mom and the baby," Dad said.

"May I go along?" I asked excitedly, and shoved my books aside.

"It's a school day tomorrow. Anyway, there isn't much room in the pickup—with all the baby's things. Why don't you stay here and get the place ready for your mom? Al, would you light a fire in the fireplace? And Heather, straighten up around here a bit. We don't want little Joseph Alfred Ames to think his new family is a bunch of slobs."

Dad laughed to take the sting away, but he had hurt my feelings. I thought I'd done a good job of keeping things picked up and doing the cooking and going to school, especially when my leg hurt so bad. Of course, Dad didn't know that I was in pain.

When they finally got back from the hospital, I was half-asleep. Mom looked tired, but happy. Grandpa Al took the baby from Dad, and you'd have thought he was holding the crown prince of England.

I went over to get a close-up look at Joey. Dad had been raving about how beautiful the baby was, so I expected him to be cuter. To me, he looked pretty pathetic.

I watched Mom put the baby in the new bassinet in her bedroom. Actually, he didn't look so bad now. *I could get used to him*, I thought. I'd saved enough to buy a little washable teddy bear. I got it out and started to put it beside Joey.

"Heather, no!" Mom said. "I need to check

it out to see if it's safe. Anyway, he's too little for it now."

"Oh . . . sure." I took the bear in my arms. "Okay, I guess I'll go to bed. I'm pretty tired."

Mom gave me a peck on the cheek, but I could tell that her mind was elsewhere. "Good night, honey. Thanks for taking such good care of everything. It's good to be home."

Feeling better, I headed for my room. Maybe a baby wouldn't be so bad, after all.

Wrong!

I hardly got any sleep that night. How can a little thing like that make so much noise for such a long time? My room is clear on the other side of the living room, but I could still hear him howling.

The next day after school, the Stars came over to see Joey. He was asleep, but Mom let us creep into the room to look at him.

"Oh, he's darling," Denise said.

She'd think Dracula was cute.

"Look at all that hair," April said. "I could almost give him a perm."

I think April has permanent wave solution in her veins instead of blood.

Jill was looking at him critically. "He'll be lucky if there are no complications because your mother is so old."

Sometimes Jill irritates me. Just because her dad's a veterinarian, she acts as if she

36

knows everything about medicine.

"He looks healthy to me," Ginny said. "I hope I have a bunch of babies some day."

She wouldn't hope that for long if she had to listen to them yell at night.

All I wanted to do was sit down. "Let's go get something to drink," I said.

We took cans of cola and some chocolate marshmallow cookies to my room. The others sat on the floor. I usually did, too. But I knew it would be too hard to get up again, so I sat on the bed.

"I'm getting nervous about Saturday," April said. "I hope I don't blow the tournament."

At least no one expected anything of her. Everyone was sure I'd do well. But I hadn't bowled in a couple of weeks. And every time I put weight on my knee, I thought I'd fall on my face.

"How should we celebrate?" Denise asked.

"We'd better win first," I said. "Doug says the Ridgefield Rockets are really good."

"Heather?" Mom called from the bedroom. "I need your help."

"Sorry, guys," I said.

April looked at her fancy new watch. "That's okay. There's a soap opera I want to see. I can still catch the end of it."

"I have homework," Ginny said. "Come on, Denise, I'll help you with your algebra."

They let themselves out, and I hurried into the bedroom. Joey was screaming. Mom put her hand over the mouthpiece of the phone. "Heather, I'm taking an order. Will you please take Joey into the nursery and change him?"

Mom had shown me how to change Joey, but I'd never done it by myself. I picked him up and carried him into my old room. I laid him on the changing table and managed to get a clean diaper on him. But when I picked him up again, a pain like a hot, sharp, twisting knife shot up my right arm.

I almost dropped Joey. He started screaming again. The near-fall must have scared him as much as it had me. For a minute I just stood there shaking.

Mom came in then. "What did you do to him, for heaven's sake?"

"Nothing," I said. "But I don't ever want to change him again."

Mom didn't say anything for a second. Her lips thinned into a straight line, the way they do when she's annoyed. "Take the wet diaper and put it in the garbage pail. Then wash your hands and peel some potatoes for dinner."

I didn't say anything about my arm. I guess I couldn't blame Mom for being angry. But if I told her the truth, she might not let me bowl in the tournament.

The next morning I was stiff all over. My

neck hurt. At first I thought I'd just slept wrong, but the pain didn't go away. I rubbed on some cream that was supposed to help sore muscles. Then I went into Mom's room. "Mom?" I croaked. "I think I'm getting the flu. I ache all over. Can I stay home today?"

She gave me a long, suspicious look, but then sighed. "All right. But don't go near the baby. All I need is two sick children."

Ordinarily she would have taken my temperature and checked my throat right away. But she was too busy with Joey. I went back to bed, but I couldn't find a comfortable position. My neck hurt, my right arm still felt as if a hot knife were digging into it, and my knee was swollen and sore. In fact, I felt rotten all over. When Mom finally came up to check on me, I pretended I was asleep. She didn't bother me.

Staying in bed for a day must have helped. On Saturday I woke up with no pain at all, just a little stiffness.

At breakfast I told Mom I was over the flu. "I feel good enough to go to the tournament today."

She shot me a quick look. "It's amazing how kids get better on weekends. If you were trying to get out of going to school or helping around here, don't think you'll get away with it again."

"Mom, I wasn't! I felt awful."

"All right. But before you go, I want you to

vacuum and dust the living room."

I had planned to go next door and bowl for a while, but I sure wasn't going to argue. "No problem," I said. "Denise's brother won't pick me up until 11:00."

"All right, honey." She gave me a kiss. "I'm sorry I've been impatient with you. It's just that I'm so tired. Good luck today. Bowl a 300 game."

I'd be happy if I could just make my average.

* * * * *

The bowling alley in Ridgefield was larger and fancier than Doug's place, but it wasn't as friendly. It was crowded with spectators. We were bowling against three other teams, but the Ridgefield Rockets was the only team we were worried about.

We were wearing jeans and matching blue shirts with a star embroidered on the back. Mine looked more like a starfish that had lost one arm. Needlework isn't one of my talents.

Doug had come along to keep score. He sat down beside me while I was changing into my bowling shoes. "You haven't been practicing. Is your knee okay?"

"I feel pretty good today, but for the last two days I've hurt all over. And I'm so stiff in the mornings I can hardly move."

"You'd better go back to the doctor," Doug said.

"I will. I was afraid old Cornball would tell me I couldn't bowl today."

"You could do some permanent damage. It's not worth it." His voice was harsh. "I ought to know."

Doug was talking about his dad. Mr. Warren had been a linebacker for the Los Angeles Rams. He'd played in a playoff game with a minor back injury. During the game he was seriously injured. He spent the rest of his life in a wheelchair. He died of a kidney infection three years ago.

I nodded. "I'll be careful."

"Good luck, Heather. Bowl 'em over," Doug said.

"Thanks." I was starting to get nervous now. Normally I didn't worry much, but I was afraid my stupid knee might give out.

We each took a practice shot, then we began. Ginny bowled first, because her average was second best. I was glad I bowled last. It gave me a chance to get rid of the butterflies before it was my turn.

Going into the third game, we were a few pins ahead. April was doing great, and I was just a little under my average. Feeling more and more confident, I got up to bowl. I needed a strike. I sent the ball down the alley. I was so sure I'd rolled a strike and knocked down all the pins that I started back to my seat. Then I heard a groan from the Stars and looked back. I couldn't believe it. The ten pin was still standing.

I waited for my ball to come back, then picked it up. With no warning, a jagged pain ripped through my arm. The ball dropped with a thud and rolled toward Doug.

He picked up the ball and brought it to me. "What's wrong?" he whispered.

"It's my elbow." I tried not to show how much pain I felt.

I took the ball in both hands, but it dropped again and nearly hit him on the foot.

"I can't do it!" I cried.

The Stars crowded around me. "You have to," Jill said. "We're ahead."

If I dropped out, we'd have to use the lowest score of my opposite, the fifth bowler on the Rockets team. "It won't be so bad," I said. "My opposite has good scores."

"Why does this have to happen now!" April moaned. "I'm doing so well for a change."

Denise came over and put her arm around me. "What's wrong?"

"Heather, you're worse than Chrissy Aldrich with your complaining," Ginny said angrily.

"I'm sorry. I'm really sorry," I cried, and

rushed off toward the restroom.

"Leave her alone," Doug said as I left.

They left me alone, all right. On the way home hardly anyone said a word. I was glad. I was in too much pain to talk.

We'd lost the tournament by three points. The Rockets won the trophy for high series and high game. April won for most improved. Her win was the only bright spot in the day.

When we got back to my place, Doug and I both got out of the car. He took my bowling bag for me.

"I'm sorry I let you down," I told my friends, who were probably no longer my friends at all.

Everyone avoided my eyes.

"See you," Denise said.

"Sure . . ." I was almost in tears. "See you."

Doug walked with me to the stairs. His face was red with anger. "Some friends you have there. Don't they know you're hurting?"

"No. You heard Ginny. Nobody likes someone who complains all the time. Look how they talk about Chrissy."

"That's dumb."

"I guess you're right," I said tiredly. "But they're mad at me, anyhow."

Doug handed me the bag, and I took it in my left hand. "Can you make it upstairs?" he asked.

"Sure, my leg feels okay. Thanks, Doug."

He waited while I climbed slowly up the million steps. At the landing I turned and gave a feeble wave. At least Doug was still my friend.

I could hardly open the door. Mom was in the kitchen, fixing baby formula. "Well, how did it go?" she asked.

"We lost," I said.

"Oh, honey, I'm sorry. But there's always the next tournament," Mom said gently.

I nodded. "I know."

"As soon as you put your things away, will you please toss a load of Joey's dirty clothes in the washer for me? And then you could scrape some carrots for dinner."

My mouth felt as if I'd been eating some of Joey's baby powder. I crossed to the sink to get a glass of water. But I couldn't turn on the faucet with my right hand. I gave a little groan.

"What's the matter?" Mom wanted to know.

"It's my wrist. Something's wrong with it."

"I see," Mom said. "You feel well enough to go bowling, but I suppose you feel too bad to help fix dinner. Didn't I tell you not to try to pull any tricks on me?"

I burst into tears and ran to my room. When Mom didn't even come in to find out what was wrong, I knew she must be really angry.

Later, Mom and Dad came to my room and opened the door. I pretended to be asleep again. I heard them talking in the hall.

"What's wrong with her?" Dad asked.

"I'm afraid she's jealous of the baby. It's my fault. I haven't given her much attention lately. And I've been pretty impatient with her. Most of the time she's so grown up that I forget she's only 13."

"It's my fault, too," Dad said. "All I do is brag about Joey. I'll try to find more time for her."

I felt guilty, so in a little while I went out to the living room.

"Hi, sweetheart," Mom said. "I saved you some dinner."

"I'm not hungry. I have to talk to you."

"Come on over here." Mom patted the couch.

I shook my head. "It's too hard for me to get up off the couch. Mom, Dad, I—I don't think I had the flu."

"I suspected you weren't really sick," Mom said. "It's all right. We understand."

"No, you don't. There's something wrong with me—really wrong. We lost the tournament because I couldn't use my right arm. Sometimes my neck hurts. Sometimes my knee or elbow hurts, and they get swollen." Tears welled up in my eyes. "Oh, Mom, what's wrong with me?"

Four

DR. Cornball was on vacation. His answering machine said he'd be back in three days, and then gave a number for a doctor in Ridgefield.

As Mom put down the phone, she gave a disgusted sigh. "The doctor's out of town. Maybe I should take you to Ridgefield or North Bay."

"It's okay," I said. I wasn't all that anxious to find out I had something awful like multiple sclerosis or bone cancer—the kind of diseases they have telethons for.

On Monday I was so stiff that it was hard for me to pull myself out of bed. But after a long, hot shower, I felt better. Grandpa Al drove me the few blocks to school in his car, because I had trouble stepping up into the cab of our pickup.

"Why didn't you tell me you were feeling poorly, Heatherbee?" he asked.

"You've been busy helping out in the store.

Anyway, you'd just tell me I was being a big baby."

"Well, are you?"

"I don't think so."

"I don't either. If you were a baby, you'd stay home from school."

"Thanks, Grandpa. I'm going to get out of gym, though," I said. Even the thought of the dumb exercises we had to do hurt.

When he dropped me off in front of the school I saw the Stars sitting on the steps. As soon as they saw me, they came running up, all talking at once.

"Heather," Denise said, "we're so sorry."

"We were jerks," April said.

"Why didn't you tell us you were in pain Saturday?" Jill asked.

"I wanted to, but you'd have thought I was a complainer. Hey, wait a minute. How'd you find out?"

"Doug told us," Ginny answered. "In fact, he told us off."

"What's the pain like?" Jill wanted to know, as if she were a doctor.

"It's kind of like when you hit your crazy bone and have a bad toothache at the same time."

Denise put her arm around me. "Is there anything we can do?"

I grinned happily. "You already have. I was

47

afraid you'd all stay mad at me."

"You're the one who should be mad," April said.

"Not really. Even my mom figured I was faking. She thought I was jealous of Joey."

"I wouldn't blame you if you were," Ginny said with a grimace. "When my little sister was born, I threw away some of her toys."

The bell rang, and we all headed for class. I did all right, except it was hard to write. My hand wouldn't work very well. And after sitting for nearly an hour, I could hardly get up.

When it was time for gym class, I went up to Ms. Harris. That's what we have to call her— Mzzz Harris.

"May I go to the library this period?" I asked. "I have a sore knee and arm and—"

Ms. Harris didn't even bother to look at me. "Everybody needs exercise. We're doing floor exercises today."

We had them every day. Or worse yet, we played dumb kid games. She never lets us play basketball or soccer or other team sports.

"But there's something really wrong—" I began. She cut me off again. I don't think that anyone has ever managed to finish a whole sentence with her.

"Bring a note from your doctor," she said and started to walk away.

"But he's out of—"

"Change your clothes, Heather. You're holding up the whole class."

I gritted my teeth, but I changed my clothes. It wouldn't be so bad if we were training for gymnastics, but she had us doing little kid stuff like the rabbit hop and the kangaroo jump. I mean—really!

But today even hops and jumps hurt my knee and neck. Then we did some tumbling— just simple forward and backward rolls. But the tumbling hurt even worse than the hops and jumps. All the time I was doing the stupid exercises, I was picturing Mzzz Harris as a bowling pin. I was throwing strike after strike. Each time the ball would hit her, she'd fall over with a crash and roll into the gutter.

I was almost sorry when gym period was over.

* * * * *

Mom couldn't go with me to see the doctor, so I asked the Stars to come along.

As I sat huddled in the corner of the couch, I only half listened to what they were saying. The night before, I had started running a temperature, and my pulse was going like a machine gun.

Dr. Cornball didn't have a patient in his office, but it was a good 15 minutes before

Miss Redfern led me in to see him.

"Well, well, Heather, my child. What brings you here today?"

"A while back you looked at my knee. You said it was strained and told me to take aspirin and put cold packs on it. It helped a little, but now I hurt all over."

Nurse Redfern took me behind a screen. I had to put on a paper gownlike thing that was cold and scratchy. I got up on the table, trying to keep the stupid paper gown from tearing.

This time the doctor did a more thorough examination—punching and poking me and asking all sorts of questions. When he was finally finished, I got dressed again and sat on the edge of the table.

"What—" I cleared my throat nervously. "What do you think's wrong with me?"

He didn't say anything for a minute, and I thought he hadn't heard me. "What do you think?"

"Well, your joints are inflamed. I'm not sure why. It might just be growing pains or maybe rheumatism," he said. "I want you to take higher doses of aspirin and keep it up for a few weeks."

"Why aspirin again?"

"As I said, your joints are inflamed. The aspirin should give you some relief."

"But you don't think I have something

terrible—like bone cancer?"

"There's no indication of that," he said kindly.

I can't tell you how relieved I was. My knee and arm didn't seem to hurt as much as when I'd come into the office.

"Now, don't you worry," he said. "Every third patient I see has a few stiff joints." He reached for a sucker.

"Doctor, I have four friends waiting for me," I said, keeping a straight face. "May I have a sucker and a balloon for each of them?"

* * * * *

After only a week or so I felt almost as well as I had before I fell. It was so nice to feel good again. From now on, I wasn't going to take good health for granted. Dr. Cornwell, I'll never call you Cornball again.

I even had enough energy to help with Joey. I couldn't believe how fast he was growing. And every day he learned something new.

I started training with Doug again. Although I felt strong, he made me start out slowly. While he ran, I walked. He'd run ahead, then come back and walk with me. By Christmas I could do a mile or two. I figured with more time to train, I'd be back running soon.

Christmas was wonderful, the best I can ever

remember. I got a new running outfit and a walkabout radio. But the best present of all was from Grandpa Al. He gave me his old stopwatch.

Since I felt so good, I kept forgetting to take the aspirin. I figured I was cured.

But one morning just after Valentine's Day, I woke up stiff again. And my neck hurt. The next day I felt okay, and I felt fine for a couple of weeks. But then it started all over again. Sometimes my elbow and knee hurt a lot. I tried not to let on, but by late April I couldn't hide the pain. And I was running out of excuses to give Doug and the Stars.

Mom took me back to Dr. Cornwell. She wanted to know why I kept getting sick.

He shook his head. "I'm not really sure," he said. "I think you'd better see the doctor in Ridgefield—a young fellow—name's Mason. He'll probably take some laboratory tests."

Miss Redfern called Dr. Mason and set up an appointment for me in two weeks.

As Mom and I left the office, I felt discouraged. I'd said I wouldn't take good health for granted—but I had. Mom gave me a quick hug. "Honey, it might not get any worse. Try to keep a positive attitude."

Easy for her to say.

Five

THE next day, a big storm blew in—and what it blew in was our big plate-glass window in the store. It sounded like an explosion. We were watching TV, and we all rushed downstairs. The wind was whistling through a gaping hole and blowing cans of chicken soup and boxes of cereal down the street. Grandpa and I got soaked trying to save some of the cans.

"Get in here," Mom called. "You'll both catch your death of cold."

I stood shivering as I watched Dad get out the ladder and the same piece of plywood he used every year to board up the window.

Grandpa Al and Mom held the wood in place while Dad pounded in nails.

"Won't hold," Grandpa predicted.

"It's held before," Dad said with a touch of irritation in his voice. He hates to have people tell him how to do things.

"Here, I'll show you," Grandpa said, and let

go of his side of the plywood. The nails didn't hold. "There! Didn't I tell you?" Grandpa said smugly.

Mom and I looked at each other and tried our best not to smile. Dad and Grandpa go on like this all the time.

"Heather, you'd better get back upstairs and change out of those wet clothes," Mom said. "And see if Joey's all right."

I figured Dad would want Grandpa out of the way, too. "Grandpa Al, how about a game of two-handed pinochle?" I asked. Grandpa can never resist pinochle.

Grandpa and I went upstairs, and I changed into my pajamas and robe. I still felt chilled, though. Grandpa turned on the radio while we cleared the dishes. All the roads south of Rocky Cove were closed from mud slides. Several beachfront houses had been destroyed by the high surf.

The waves were crashing up against the banks so loudly, we could hear them from clear up here, nearly a half mile away. The wind howled and whistled against the windows, and I was glad Grandpa was with me.

Joey was still asleep in his playpen. He was almost six months old now and was getting really cute. I'd never tell anybody, but when he grins at me, I could just hug him to pieces.

When Mom and Dad came back upstairs,

Grandpa said he was leaving. "Why don't you stay all night on the sofa bed in the living room?" Dad suggested. "Al, it's terrible outside."

"A little wind and rain won't kill me. But that lumpy excuse for a bed might."

I figured Grandpa was still a bit miffed at Dad over the window. "Grandpa Al, we could build a fire, and you could tell me some stories."

He tousled my hair. "That's a tempting offer, Heatherbee, but I'm going home."

He bundled up in his yellow slicker and hat. "This storm is a puny little thing," he said. "You should have been around in the winter of '31. Now *that* was a humdinger of a storm." As he went out the back door, he gave a parting shot. "Call me, Howard, if you need help with that window downstairs."

Dad stood on the landing until Grandpa crossed the muddy field between the store and the bowling alley and made it back up the stairs to his place. "Now, I know where you and Heather get your stubbornness," Dad said to Mom.

I got into bed and turned on my radio to cover the sound of the wind. My face felt hot. I touched my wrist and knew my pulse was galloping again.

I had just fallen asleep when I heard another

crash from downstairs. Only this time it wasn't glass shattering. Grandpa Al had been right about the plywood not holding.

I got up to help, but Dad said, "You stay up here, Heather."

I was glad. I wasn't feeling so great.

I climbed back in my nice warm bed. I'd almost dozed off again when I heard a yell and a loud thud. "Heather," Mom shouted from the stairs. "Call Dr. Cornwell. Your father's fallen off the ladder. I think his arm's broken. Hurry!"

I looked up the number and dialed. But I got the answering machine. He was out of town again. I went downstairs to tell Mom and Dad. The plywood board was in place, but Dad was sitting on the floor, holding his arm and looking sick.

Mom was kneeling beside him. "I don't need a doctor," he said.

"Don't be silly, Howard. I'm sure your arm's broken. I'm not waiting for Dr. Cornwell to return. I'm taking you to Ridgefield now."

"The road might be washed out," I said. "Grandpa and I heard there's a mud slide south of here."

"There shouldn't be any problem between here and Ridgefield," Dad said. His voice sounded faint and filled with pain. "Heather, please get my coat and hat."

"Bring two blankets," Mom put in. "And get one of my big scarves. I'll try to make a sling."

"Should I call Grand—"

"No!" Dad said quickly. "I don't want to hear him say I told you so."

I got the stuff Mom and Dad had asked for and brought it downstairs. As Mom started giving me instructions, the lights flickered, dimmed, then came on strong again.

"Heather, you'd better put some wood in the fireplace," Dad said, his voice sounding weak. "If the electricity goes off, the furnace won't work."

"You can sleep in our bed," Mom told me. "You can hear Joey if he wakes up. His bottles are in the refrigerator."

"I know, Mom. Don't worry about me. I'll get out the flashlight and candles."

As they were leaving, Mom said, "We should be back before it's time to open the store. But if we're not, call your grandfather."

"And see if Henry can work for a week or so," Dad added.

I kissed them good-bye. "Don't worry about anything here," I told them confidently.

But as I slowly climbed the stairs, my stomach felt hollow. My hands were damp and clammy on the railing, and my head was throbbing.

The stairs seemed a mile long. Upstairs, the

wind sounded even louder than in the market. I decided to call Grandpa. The phone rang a dozen times, but he didn't answer. When he's asleep, a bomb could go off, and he wouldn't hear it.

I put more wood on the fire and checked to be sure the screen was closed. Then I got out the candles and flashlights. As I crept into Mom and Dad's king-size bed, I felt very alone. I was tempted to bring Joey into bed with me, but I was afraid I'd wake him up.

I lay there listening to the wind howl, then covered my head with blankets, leaving only my nose out so I could breathe.

* * * * *

I must have fallen asleep fairly quickly. In my dream I was lost in Alaska. The blizzard roared around me as I stumbled on. My feet, wrapped in old rags, were sore and bleeding, leaving a trail of blood behind me. I heard a growl and turned to see a huge polar bear. It stood on its hind legs and growled again.

I woke up with a start. The growling was really Joey howling. A tree branch was banging against the window.

I tried to raise up, but I could hardly move. A hundred burning daggers stabbed me. Joey was screaming now. I'd never heard him cry like that before. Something was wrong.

Groaning with the effort, I pulled myself to the edge of the bed. I held my breath and let myself drop to the floor. I was stunned for a second, then I inched my way to the door and into the nursery. "Joey, it's okay," I said. "Don't cry. It's okay." But he just screamed louder. I knew I couldn't lift him out of the crib. I had to get help.

I managed to get to the phone in the hall, but it was too much effort to lift my arms high enough to reach it. I yanked the cord, and the phone fell off, almost hitting me on the shoulder. After struggling with it, I finally got the receiver to my ear.

The line was dead.

I had to get help. I had to get to Grandpa.

I tried to pull myself to my feet, but my legs wouldn't hold me very well. I kept falling. Salty tears of pain rolled down my face.

Joey's crying gave me the strength to make it out to the kitchen. Trying to reach the doorknob hurt so much I nearly blacked out. I rested for a minute, then tried again, using my right hand to push my left arm higher.

The door opened inward, and I had to move out of the way. Finally, I was on the landing. The rain had stopped, but the wind was still blowing. I shivered from the cold. "I'll get—help—Joey—" I kept saying over and over.

It was early, and there was no one on the street to hear me. The bowling alley was close. But at this hour it was closed, and Doug and his mother would be in their apartment clear on the other end of the building. Grandpa's apartment was closer—if only I could get there.

I looked down at all those open wooden steps, then began to inch backward down the long flight. Every few minutes I had to stop. My heart was pounding loudly. "Just a few more—just a few—" I gasped.

At the bottom, I lay there, panting for breath. I could still hear Joey crying. "Joey— it's—okay." I had to go on. I just had to.

As I made my way out into the mud, I wanted to give up. I was shaking so badly I could hardly move. Finally, I made it to the foot of Grandpa's stairs. "Grandpa!" I shouted. "Help me!"

Gathering every bit of strength I had left, I began to pull myself up the steps. "Grandpa— help. Help—Joey . . ."

My knees and arms scraped against the rough wood. Gasping with every breath, I fought my way up two steps. My entire body was filled with flaming, agonizing pain. I clawed at the next step, lost my balance, and fell back. The world spun around me—then blackness. . . .

Six

I slowly opened my eyes to see Grandpa sitting beside my bed. If it hadn't been for the awful pain, I'd have thought I was having a nightmare. But no dream could hurt this much.

"How—" I gasped. "How did I get here?"

"I found you," Doug said.

I tried to turn my head to see him, but the effort was too much.

"You were trying to climb up Grandpa Al's stairs, and you were moaning, 'Get Joey.'"

"Is he all right?" I asked weakly.

"Sleeping like a baby," Grandpa said, trying to be funny. "It was just a bellyache. He's fine now."

I sank back, relieved. "And how's Dad? Did Mom call, or is the phone still out?"

"No, the phone's back on now. Your mother called a little while ago. Your father just has a hairline fracture. He'll be all right. She said they'd be home soon."

I frowned, trying to think. Even thinking hurt. "I can't remember much. How long have I been asleep?"

"A couple of hours, maybe," Grandpa told me. "How do you feel, honey?"

"Cold—and hot." I tried to push off the covers, but I didn't have enough strength. "Grandpa, please take off the blanket. It's too heavy."

He did as I asked, but even the sheet was too much weight. It hurt my feet.

"How about a nice cup of hot cocoa?" Grandpa asked.

I started to shake my head, but stopped as pain knifed through my neck. "Just water, please. My mouth's dry."

Grandpa lifted my head enough to hold a glass of water to my lips. After a few sips, I sank back on the pillow, totally exhausted.

"Did you call the doctor?" I asked.

"I tracked old Dr. Cornball down," Doug said. "He'll be here in a little while." Doug came over close to the bed and looked at me for a minute. "Heather, you sure scared me."

I gave him a weak smile. "I was just trying to get out of going to school."

"School! I'm going to be late," he moaned. "See you later. Hope you start feeling better. Bye," he said, and rushed out.

After Doug left, Grandpa went to the

nursery to see about Joey. I guess I must have dozed off. The next thing I knew, I heard Mom, Dad, and Dr. Cornwell talking about me. I pretended to be asleep.

"Her neck and legs are sore," Mom said, and I could hear the fear in her voice. "It's not—not something like meningitis, is it?"

"I don't think we should talk in front of her," Dad said. "She might wake up."

They walked out of the room, so I didn't hear the doctor's answer.

* * * * *

Dr. Cornwell called Dr. Mason in Ridgefield and got us an appointment in two days. I was too sick to want to move. Mom had to help me get to the bathroom. She practically carried me.

"Will you be all right for a few minutes?" she asked. "I have to dress Joey."

"I'll be okay until you get back."

But when I tried to lift my arm to brush my teeth, all I could do was stand there leaning against the sink, tears streaming down my face.

I hardly recognized the person in the mirror. My hair was limp and straggly, and my face was pale. Even my brown eyes looked washed out. It's weird how pain makes your face get all tight and pinched.

"You're a real beauty," I said to my reflection. "You should try out for Miss Rocky Cove next summer."

The Stars came over after school. Ginny brought my assignments and books. April brushed my hair and braided it so it would stay out of my face. Jill proceeded to tell me she thought I had some 15-letter disease that I'd never heard of. Frankly, I think she just made it up.

Denise tried to cheer me up. "You should have seen Mzzz Harris today. Somebody put itching powder in her gym shorts." Denise and the others laughed. "She was wriggling and squirming. We thought it was some new exercise at first."

I tried to laugh, too. "It's a good thing I wasn't there. She'd probably have blamed me."

They changed the subject and began talking about guys and a new video that Jill had seen. I was happy to see my friends, but trying to be cheerful took too much effort. I was glad when Mom came in to say I needed to rest.

When the Stars were gone, I leaned back against the cushions, more exhausted than I'd let on.

Doug came over after dinner, but we didn't talk much. He brought a tape, and we listened to music. Doug's easy to be around. Lots of times when we're running, we don't say a word for miles.

Running. Will I ever run again? At that moment, I really didn't care.

On the day of my appointment, I felt awful.

"Mom, I'm so stiff I can hardly move!"

Mom sighed and seemed upset. "Take a long hot shower, honey, and maybe you'll feel better."

Mom's advice was good. My joints loosened up some after the shower. But I couldn't raise my arm high enough to brush my hair. And when I tried to pull a sweater over my head, the pain was so bad that I almost screamed out loud.

I limped out to the living room to ask for Mom's help, but stopped as I heard Mom and Dad talking about me. I leaned up against the wall and listened.

"Howard," Mom was saying, "I'm just about at my wits' end. I don't know what to do about Heather." Mom sighed heavily. "One minute I'm ready to fly her to the Mayo Clinic, and the next minute, I'm sure her problems are psychological."

"I know," Dad said. "Sometimes she's more trouble than Joey."

The words slashed like a knife. I didn't want to be trouble to anybody.

"It's just so frustrating. One day she's fine, the next she's crying. I don't know whether to baby her or spank her."

"I know what you mean," Dad added. "I came into the kitchen yesterday. She was standing in the middle of a bunch of glass, crying. At first I thought she'd gotten mad and deliberately broken a glass. But I really think she dropped it because her hands hurt."

"Heather and I have never been able to talk much. It would help if she'd just open up," Mom said, her voice sounding hurt. "She shuts me out. She won't even talk to her grandpa."

Didn't they know some things were too hard to talk about?

"Kids go through stages like this where they put a wall around themselves. She'll snap out of it. It's just a phase."

"I hope you're right . . ."

I didn't want to hear any more. As I limped back to the bathroom, tears scalded my eyes. I wished I could just go away and never be any trouble to anybody ever again.

I managed to struggle into the sweater, and went back out to the livng room. I stood in the hall for a second, took a deep breath, and straightened my shoulders. Trying not to limp, I went in. "I'm all ready," I said brightly. "Let's go."

I dreaded the drive to Ridgefield, but by the

time we got to the doctor's office, the pain was only a dull ache.

The waiting room was full. A little kid had the sniffles. And one little boy was covered with red bumps. All I needed was to catch the measles or chicken pox.

Dr. Mason made me move all my joints, and he poked at them. He took my temperature, and it was a little high.

"We'll do some blood tests today," he said. "And I want you to have X rays taken. We need to see what's going on in your joints. You might have arthritis."

Arthritis! What a joke. That was what old people got. I didn't think this doctor was much better than old Cornball.

"Continue taking the aspirin," Dr. Mason said. He prescribed a little higher dose than Dr. Cornwell had. And he said to take the aspirin every day, whether I was feeling good or bad. He also suggested hot showers and told me to get plenty of rest.

We made an appointment to come back in three weeks. As we were leaving, the nurse handed me some brochures on exercise. Some of the ones for the hands seemed really silly— like the exercises Mzzz Harris made us do. They had names like Creeper, Flicker, Chopper, and Rolling Pin.

On the way home, Mom and I didn't say

anything for a while. Finally she said, "Well, at least he didn't think it was anything very serious."

*   *   *   *   *

The aspirin didn't help much. At times, it hurt to do almost anything. And some days, I could barely walk.

Mom called Dr. Mason and told him I didn't seem to be improving.

"What did he say?" I wanted to know.

She hung up the phone in frustration. "He said to give the aspirin more time to work!" She came over to me and hugged me. "I'm sorry, honey. Try to hang in there a little longer."

I hated going to school on the bad days. I had trouble keeping up with my assignments. I hurt so much I couldn't concentrate. I hated having the kids see me shuffle along, flat-footed, stiff-kneed—ugly. It was hard to stand in line in the cafeteria or to use the restrooms.

One day the Stars were going out of the cafeteria after lunch. Three seventh-graders blocked our way and whistled at April. We ignored them and stepped off the cement path onto the grass. The uneven ground was harder to walk on, and I limped badly.

"What's the matter with Heather? Is she a

cripple?" Chip Foley called out.

My insides shriveled.

Denise whirled around. "You shut your mouth!" she shouted.

"Who's going to make me?"

"We are," the Stars said in unison, and started moving toward the boys. Jill jabbed her finger in front of Chip's face. "You ever call her that again, and you'll be sorry."

He made a face of mock terror. "Oh, we're scared to death, aren't we, guys?"

I felt awful standing there. "Forget it," I said to the Stars. "They aren't worth it."

"Yeah, come on, Chip," Tom said, pulling him away. "Don't be such a jerk."

Chip made some remark I couldn't hear, then he strutted off.

Tom and Gary looked a little embarrassed. "Sorry," they mumbled, and took off after Chip.

Denise put her arm around me. "Don't let him get to you, Heather. Some people don't have any sense."

"It'll take more than that creep to get me down," I said.

I really tried not to let anyone bother me. Grandpa says that because they're embarrassed, kids make fun of people with any kind of problem. I think kids do it because they're just plain stupid.

I watched TV a lot, but every time Mom or Dad came into the room, I'd pretend I was doing the exercises. Even the easy ones hurt. I tried not to let on how much pain I was in. Just putting on a blouse or tying my shoes was a struggle. And buttons drove me crazy. Now I knew how old people must feel.

Doug came over almost every day to help me with my homework. But some days, even holding a book or pencil was awful. I had to use my left hand, and nobody could read my sloppy writing.

I was too tired most of the time to want to do anything. It was hard to keep up a front. Nobody seemed to understand how I felt. But then—I didn't understand how I felt, either. I hated the way I looked, and I hated myself.

I'd been trying to tough it out, but I was getting discouraged. The aspirin didn't seem to be doing much good. *I'm never going to get any better*, I thought. I just huddled on my bed, crying. I didn't want to read or watch TV or even talk to anybody.

One Friday, Grandpa knocked on my door, then came in.

"Heatherbee, how about a game of checkers?"

"No, thanks," I mumbled, and turned away so I couldn't see the hurt on his face.

"Well, maybe tomorrow." He closed the

door softly. I knew he was disappointed.

I could hear him talking to Mom in the living room. Mom had to talk loudly to make Grandpa hear.

"I don't like the way our girl's acting," Grandpa said. "It's not like her to hide in her room."

"Oh, Dad, I'm worried sick about her. She seems to be getting worse. The doctor says to give the aspirin a chance to work, but I can't sit here and watch her hurt."

Mom sounded as if she was about to cry. I guess I hadn't realized how much she worried about me.

"Maybe we should just bundle her up and take her to San Francisco. Surely, there's somebody who can help her!" Mom said angrily.

"Take it easy, Sheila," Grandpa said. "She goes back to the doctor in a week or so, doesn't she?"

"Yes, but she's been to two doctors, and neither of them has helped her. I can't stand it. Howard doesn't say much, but I know it almost kills him to see Heather in pain."

Oh, Mom, I'm sorry. I'm sorry I'm so much trouble. I wanted to rush in to Mom and Grandpa, and tell them not to worry—that I was going to be okay. But I was afraid I'd never be well again. So, instead, I buried my

71

head in my pillow and cried myself to sleep.

*　*　*　*　*

The next day, Doug came over. I was just sitting on the couch, staring into space.

"Hi," he said cheerfully. "How's it going?"

"It's not," I said, wishing he'd go. I just wanted to be left alone.

"Want to go to the track meet? Mom said she'd drive you there."

"No, thanks."

"I'm running the mile, and I'm in the relay. I thought you might like—"

"No," I said sharply, cutting him off. Why did he have to talk about running?

"Boy, you're a barrel of fun these days, Heather." He was scowling at me. "What are you going to do—sit in this room and mope around for the rest of your life?"

"It's my life." I blinked back the tears that threatened, and turned my face to the wall.

Seven

AFTER school on Monday, I watched Joey. He was in his playpen, and keeping an eye on him didn't take a lot of effort.

I slumped down against the cushions, wondering if I'd ever run again.

The first woman runner is just coming into the stadium. It looks like—yes, it is, the youngest girl to ever enter the Olympic marathon—Heather Ames of the United States.

And then I was standing on the winner's platform, listening to our national anthem. I felt the gold medal on my chest, and blinked back the tears of joy and pride . . .

I'll never run again—I know it.

"Heather, are you all right?" Mom asked.

I turned away so she couldn't see my eyes. "I'm fine—just fine." My voice cracked a little, but I didn't think she noticed.

She put more toys in the playpen. "Honey, I really appreciate your watching Joey for me. It's a big help."

She had no more than left when I heard five quick knocks on the back door.

"Come in," I called in answer to the Stars' signal knock. "The door's unlocked."

They came tiptoeing in as if I were an invalid. The last couple of weeks, they'd been treating me differently—trying too hard.

"Hi, guys," I said. "What are you up to?"

It was a warm day and they were wearing shorts and T-shirts. I was covered with a quilt. I felt cold most of the time now, no matter what the weather was like.

Nobody said anything. They were fidgeting and acting embarrassed.

"Well? What are you up to?" I repeated.

"We want to know what you're going to wear to graduation," April said.

"I don't know," I said. "I might not even go." The principal had talked to me about graduation, but I'd told him the same thing. I didn't want to have everybody watch me limp across the stage.

"But you have to go," Denise said. "The Stars have done everything together since we started first grade."

"We haven't done much of anything together since I got sick," I said sourly. "Anyway, it's no big deal."

"You don't really mean that," Ginny said. "Everybody wants to go to graduation."

"Well, I don't," I said crossly. "And I don't want to talk about it. Okay?"

April walked over and sat on the arm of the couch. She touched my hair. "Boy, you need a haircut. You're really looking shaggy."

"So I'll shave my head," I said, and pulled away from April.

"Hey, Joey," Ginny said, leaning over the playpen. "You're getting so big. Does he walk yet, Heather?"

I didn't know whether she accented the word *he* on purpose or by accident, but it made me mad. "No, he doesn't walk, and I'm having trouble walking, too. Did you guys come by just to tell me how rotten I look and to remind me that I can't do a lot of things anymore?"

Jill gave me an exasperated look. "You know something, Heather, you used to be a lot of fun. But now I honestly don't care whether you even come to graduation!"

"Jill!" Denise cried. "Don't talk to her that way. You know she's sick."

"Look," I yelled, "I don't need any of you coming around just because you feel sorry for me. I don't need your pity!"

"I'm sorry," Jill said, but she didn't look at me, and she didn't sound all that sorry, either.

Tears stung my eyes. "Why don't you all just leave me alone!"

I heard a sound at the archway to the kitchen and looked up to see Grandpa and Doug standing there. I didn't know how much they'd heard, but by their faces, I guessed they'd heard plenty.

"We came to take Joey outside," Grandpa said. "Don't mind us."

"My friends were just leaving," I said coldly. "They have a lot to do."

"I'll call you," Denise said. "Maybe you'll change your mind."

I shook my head. "Don't bother. I'm not going. Period."

The girls mumbled good-byes and left in a hurry.

I hated to think that Doug had heard me. He probably thought I was awful. Well, who cared? Not me. I didn't need any of them.

Grandpa picked Joey up and headed for the back door. "Doug, I'll take the little tyke out in his stroller and meet you at the park."

. The room was warm and silent, except for the buzz of a fly and an occasional sound from the market downstairs. Doug sat on the brick ledge of the fireplace. He was staring at his hands.

I owed Doug a lot. He had come over nearly every day and worked with me.

Doug cleared his throat a couple of times. "Heather? I—uh, I'm sorry I came at a bad time."

I shrugged, then winced from the pain in my shoulder. "What did you want to talk to me about?"

"Mom and I are lining up summer leagues. I wondered if you were going to bowl with the Stars. Mom's getting the shirts made."

"You know I can't lift anything as heavy as a bowling ball."

"Maybe you can't right now, but with practice, your hand and arm will get stronger again."

"Thank you, Dr. Warren," I said sarcastically.

"If you don't start using your muscles, they'll waste away," he said.

"Oh, you sound like Jill. How do you know so much about it?"

"Because my dad went through the same thing after his injury. He couldn't use his legs, but he didn't let that stop him."

"So he was a saint. I'm not like him, and I never will be. Why don't you all just leave me alone!"

Doug got up and stood in front of the couch. Then he just looked at me for a minute and said quietly, "I never expected you to be a quitter, Heather." He turned and headed for the kitchen.

I wanted to call out, *Don't go, Doug! I'm sorry.* The words choked in my throat. I felt tears threaten, but I wasn't going to cry. I closed my eyes and held my body rigid until I heard the back door slam.

Gritting my teeth, I pulled myself up. I ignored the pain and managed the few steps to my room.

I stared at my blue ribbons and medals for a minute. What did I need with this junk? I yanked them from the wall and dumped them into the wastebasket. I pushed my bowling trophy off the desk and onto the floor. I was never going to run in a marathon or wear an Olympic gold medal and see the American flag waving over the winner's stand. Angry tears blurred my eyes.

I sank down on my bed and buried my face in the pillow. I hated myself for yelling at Doug and the Stars. They'd never want to talk to me again. I was nothing but a burden to Mom and Dad.

I couldn't keep back the hot tears any longer. The wracking sobs hurt, but I couldn't stop. In my whole life I'd never felt so awful and so alone.

* * * * *

The next afternoon, while Mom had Joey downstairs in the market, I watched a soap opera. There's one thing about soap operas— the characters' problems always seem worse than your own. Grandpa came in carrying my sweater. "Here, put this on," he said, "and no back talk."

He helped me put the sweater on, then said, "All right, Heatherbee, we're going to the park."

"I don't want to go anywhere."

But he didn't pay any attention to me. He could force me to get out of the house, but he couldn't make me like it.

"We have to tell your mother where we're going," Grandpa said, and helped me down the stairs to the market.

The place was full of customers. I hadn't been downstairs in a while. Mom came over to us. "What are you doing down here, honey?"

"It wasn't my idea," I said.

"Doug and I are taking her to the park," Grandpa told her.

Several customers hurried over.

"Sheila, what's wrong with her?" Mrs. Jensen asked.

"We aren't sure. Her joints are stiff. They think it may be arthritis," Mom answered.

"Heather looks—fine," Mrs. Murdock said. "Just fine. She's a little thin, but she doesn't look sick to me."

I hated the way people talked about me as if I weren't there. I cringed, wanting to hide somewhere.

"My neighbor's cousin has a daughter her age," Mrs. Williams said. "They couldn't figure what was ailing her, either. She took vinegar and honey every day."

"You poor little thing," Mrs. Jefferson said. "It must be awful for you not to be able to play with your little friends." She squeezed my hand, and I nearly yelled out loud. Just because nobody could see anything wrong with me, they did dumb things.

I'd grown up in the store. I was only a baby when Mom and Dad had taken over. Most of the customers had helped feed me and play with me when I was little. I knew they meant well, but the noise and the people made me want to scream, *Leave me alone!*

"Sheila," Mrs. Jensen said to Mom, "have you tried using snake venom for the child? Mr. Hennessey's mother swears by it. She couldn't move a muscle before she tried it."

"Hogwash," Grandpa muttered. "Come on, Heather." He glared at the customers. The deep line between his eyes looked like a canyon. "Let's get out of here before they turn this place into a clinic."

Mom kissed me. "Don't keep her out too long, Dad," she said to Grandpa. "Heather tires easily."

"We'll be back for dinner," he said.

Doug was waiting for us in Grandpa's car.

He got out and helped me into the front seat. The windows were open, and the air felt wonderful. I breathed in the tangy, salty smell of the sea. I began to relax a little, and the tightness in my neck and shoulders eased. I had to admit that getting outside was a good idea.

When we got to the park, Doug and I sat on benches opposite each other. I expected Grandpa to sit down beside me, but he dug his toe into the sandy dirt and cleared his throat a couple of times. "Well, if you two don't mind, I think I'll mosey on down to the beach and see if I can find some agates."

"I don't mind," Doug said, and looked at me.

I shook my head. But I wondered what those two were up to.

We didn't say anything for a bit. "Doug, I'm sorry I yelled at you yesterday," I said finally.

"You are getting to be a pain in the neck sometimes," he said.

I glanced up quickly to find him smiling. I picked at the peeling green paint on the bench. "I guess I deserve that."

"Well, you sure make it hard for people to want to help you."

"I don't want help," I lashed out, then bowed my head. "I'm sorry."

He reached out and gently took my hands in his. "Heather, I can't stand seeing you like this."

I bristled, thinking he was talking about how I looked.

He seemed to know what I was thinking. "I mean, I'm afraid you'll give up. You're a born cross-country runner. No born runner quits before the race is over."

"Did Grandpa Al coach you on what to say to me?"

He smiled sheepishly. "Well, maybe just a little. But you should listen to him. He's a pretty smart old guy."

"I just hope somebody's smart enough to help me. I go back to Dr. Mason on Monday. Surely he'll figure out something to make me feel better."

"That sounds more like the Heather I know." Doug got up and stretched. "I see Grandpa Al coming back. Do you mind if I run for a while? I didn't get out this morning."

"No," I said. But I did mind. Maybe I was being selfish, but I hated to be reminded that I might never run along this beach again, never have that wonderful feeling of seeming to fly over the sand.

A lump swelled up in my throat. I watched Doug run down the bank to the beach. At the bottom he turned and waved. I waved back, even though it hurt my arm.

Doug was a good friend. How could I feel sorry for myself with him around? I sat there in the warm sun thinking about what he had said. *You're a born cross-country runner. No born runner quits before the race is over.*

Well, he's right, I thought. I'm not a quitter. This race isn't over yet.

And the first thing I'm going to do is go to graduation.

Eight

"DENISE," I yelled over the phone, "I'm going to try to go to graduation."

"That's great! But, Heather, I'm not deaf!"

"I'm sorry," I said with a laugh. "I get used to shouting around Grandpa Al. Anyway, what are we doing this year?"

"The principal is giving out certificates and some awards," Denise said. "Then we're having a reception for our parents—just cake and punch. Afterward, we're having a party in the gym. The Stars are going to help with the decorating."

"I don't know how much I can help, but count me in."

"Boy, you sure sound better than you did yesterday."

"That's another reason I called. I—uh—I'm sorry I was such a pain."

"I don't blame you," Denise said. "I'm terrible to be around when I only have a sore throat or an earache. Hey, listen, the decorating committee's meeting tomorrow. Can you come over to the gym?"

I only had two days until graduation, but I knew I would get there even if I had to use Doug's father's wheelchair. "I'll be there."

We talked a little more about what we'd wear. When I hung up I felt happier than I had in weeks. Nobody was ever going to think of me as a quitter again.

I'd been taking the aspirin—whenever I remembered. But now I figured if I took a few extra, I'd feel better faster.

The next day, I increased the amount. On the day of graduation, I noticed ringing in my ears, but ignored it. By noon I felt really weird. When we were eating an early dinner, my head felt as if it belonged to somebody else, and my breathing sounded funny.

Mom had bought a pizza, and there's nothing I like more than pizza. But when I took a bite, it was nauseating. "Mom," I yelled, "I'm sick!"

She came running and helped me to the bathroom. I knew she was talking to me, but I couldn't make out her words.

Suddenly everything went fuzzy. "Mom, I— I—" The room began to spin, then went black.

* * * * *

I woke up in the North Bay hospital. Mom

and Dad were standing over me. "What—what—happened—?"

"Ssh," Dad said, and took my hand. "You had aspirin toxicity. But you're all right now."

I expected to be bawled out for taking so much aspirin, but Mom and Dad were great.

"What time is it?" I asked.

"8:15," Mom said.

"I've missed graduation!"

"I'm sorry, honey. We called the principal as soon as we got to the hospital. The school will mail you your certificate." Mom kept shaking her head. "Sweetheart, why did you take so many aspirin?"

"I thought it would help me get better faster."

Dr. Mason came in just then to tell us that I could be released.

"I think it would be a good idea to take her to a specialist, a pediatric rheumatologist. Dr. Matthews has an office across from this hospital. If you'd like, I can set up an appointment for you to see him as soon as possible."

The next afternoon, Mom and Dad and I were back in North Bay.

I liked Dr. Matthews right off. He was young, and he had red curly hair and a beard. And he was nice, but even more important, he seemed to know what he was doing.

First, he asked a million questions—I mean

stuff that happened to me when I was a baby, and how long I'd felt like this, and if anyone in the family had ever had arthritis or diabetes or lupus. He called it my history.

He gave me a physical examination, and I had a bunch of tests and X rays. Then an ophthalmologist checked my eyes for inflammation. I was exhausted by the time they were finished with me.

"I'm sorry this has taken so long," Dr. Matthews said. "But it's important for me to get all the details." He paused for a moment. "I think you've had so much discomfort and pain because your joints have been inflamed. That means you have arthritis. It's a type we call juvenile rheumatoid arthritis, or JRA."

"Dr. Mason said it might be arthritis, but I didn't really believe him." *Kids don't get arthritis. It has to be something else.* "I thought only old people got arthritis," I said.

"Most people think it's a disease of the elderly," the doctor said. "But children get arthritis, too—even one- and two-year-olds. At our clinic at Childrens Hospital, we take care of over 400 children who have arthritis. You have a form of JRA called polyarticular. That means 'many joints.' "

"Is it catching—like measles?" I asked.

He shook his head no.

"Then how did I get it? Was it because I

fell and hurt my knee?"

"No, but the fall might have aggravated the problem. We just don't know the cause. Sometimes arthritis comes on after a trauma or an emotional event, but most doctors don't think the event is the cause. It's an illness in which the immune system is misbehaving and attacking your joints, instead of only attacking viruses and bacteria the way it's supposed to do."

He went on with a long discussion about how the immune system works. And how, when it "misbehaves," it causes arthritis.

I was only half listening. I was wondering if I'd ever run again, when I heard Dad ask if there was a cure.

"Not in the usual sense," Dr. Matthews said gently. "But it can go into remission."

"No cure! Am I going to be like this all my life?" I asked, biting my lips so I wouldn't cry.

"The outlook for JRA is better than for rheumatoid arthritis in adults. It can usually be controlled with medication, but it will take a lot of hard work on your part, Heather."

"Hard work is no problem. Easy frazeezy, as my grandpa says. I'll be running the mile in a few months," I said to the doctor, trying to sound confident.

I looked over at Mom who sat there as if she'd been hit with a sledgehammer. "Isn't that right, Mom?"

"What—oh, yes, of course, dear."

"Heather," the doctor said, "I think the best thing right now is for you to go to Childrens Hospital to start your therapy."

A hospital! I didn't want to go to a hospital.

"We have a superior rehabilitation center there," he went on. "Heather, your muscles already have some atrophy. That's what happens when they're not used enough. They start to waste away and become useless."

"Well—whatever you think is best, Dr. Matthews," Dad said.

"But why didn't the other doctors tell us all this?" Mom asked. "I feel terrible. I should have brought her to a specialist right away."

"Don't feel guilty, Mrs. Ames. JRA is difficult to diagnose. Aspirin treatment was a good start. But it wasn't doing the job. The important thing is that Heather needs further treatment now." He turned back to me. "We want to teach you more about arthritis and start you on some range-of-motion exercises to strengthen your muscles."

I wondered if they'd have dumb names like the exercises Dr. Mason had given me.

"We'll make further plans about medication, and I think we should strongly consider putting you on gold therapy."

"Gold? You mean real gold like in my chain?" I asked, fingering my necklace.

He smiled. "Real gold . . . it's a medication made from gold salts."

"How long is she going to have arthritis?" Dad wanted to know.

"It's difficult to predict." He turned to me again. "Heather, you may have a remission. That means all the symptoms of pain and swelling will go away. A remission can last a month, years, or forever. The hardest part to deal with is that until your disease is under control, you feel achy and tired. Some days are good. Others are not so good."

I nodded. "That's it, all right. And nobody believes you." I gave Mom an I-told-you-so look.

"I'm afraid I've been guilty of that," Mom said. "At first I thought she was jealous of the baby. Heather seemed to feel bad at very convenient times. Most of the time, though, I felt like I'd been pampering her and letting her get away with too much."

Dr. Matthews nodded. "I'm sure that's very frustrating, Mrs. Ames. It's difficult to know how much you should pamper her and when you should push her." He turned to me. "Heather, that's one of the important things we'll help you with—learning which kinds of activities are good for you, and which kind you should avoid. Then you'll make the choices."

"Why do I have to go to a hospital? Can't you

just tell me what to do? I don't want to go to another doctor. I promise I'll do exactly what you say."

"I'll be at the hospital. I'm here at this office only one day a week."

If he was going to be there, maybe it wouldn't be so bad, I thought.

"We'll be teaching you many things. It will take time for you and your parents to learn to do the exercises safely and in the most effective way. In the beginning, it's hard to do the exercises all by yourself."

"Well . . . I guess I can put up with it for a little while if the hurting stops. How long will I have to stay?"

"For about eight weeks."

I turned to Mom in alarm. "But that's two months!"

"You'll be surprised how fast the time will go," Dr. Matthews told me. "You'll be too busy to even think about being homesick."

I thought about being away from everybody for two whole months. But if it made me feel better. . . .

"Stress can make you feel worse, Heather," Dr. Matthews said. "Try to keep from getting upset." He smiled. "I know that's a tough assignment. We'll arrange for you to be admitted to the hospital in one week."

Then he gave me a prescription for a new

medicine to replace the aspirin. He called it a non-steroidal, anti-inflammatory medication. If that didn't work well enough, he'd start me on gold.

I was almost afraid to ask the next question. "Dr. Matthews, will I be able to run again?"

He paused. "At the moment, it's not a good idea for you to run, because every time you do, you stir up the arthritis in your weight-bearing joints. And you make your arthritis worse."

My heart sank, and I slumped in the chair. I guess he realized how I felt, because he added, "But, Heather, if your arthritis improves enough or goes into remission, then you can run again."

"Mom! Dad! Did you hear that?" I felt a million times better than I had a few minutes ago.

"I'm going to get better," I said to the doctor. "I'm going to be a marathon runner, you know."

But deep down I was still scared.

* * * * *

"So what did the doctor say?" Denise asked.

The rest of the Stars were sitting on the floor in front of the couch where I was propped up against pillows.

"Oh, it's just something called JRA." I tried to make light of it. I didn't want to be *different*. "I'll be running and bowling before you know it." I tried to change the subject. "You should see the doctor. He's so cute. He has red—"

"But what's JRA?" Ginny asked.

"Juvenile something . . . I can't remember."

"Well, I know," Jill said. "It's juvenile rheumatoid arthritis. My aunt has rheumatoid arthritis, and her joints are all swollen out of shape. She can't walk or anything."

Denise glared at her. "You really know how to cheer a person up, Jill."

"There's no sense in Heather ignoring the facts."

"I'm not," I told her. "The doctor says most kids get along better than adults. Anyway, I'm going to the rehabilitation center in Childrens Hospital next week."

"A hospital!" April cried. "Oh, I hate hospitals. Remember when I had a broken leg? It was awful."

"I don't think this place is like a regular hospital," I said. "And guess what—I might be treated with gold—real gold."

"Wow!" April said. "You'll be worth a fortune."

"I wonder if you'll set off the metal detectors at the airport?" Jill asked.

"I don't know, but won't it be weird?"

"How long do you have to stay?" Denise asked.

"Just a couple of months. It'll be a snap."

Nobody said anything for a while, then they all jumped up at once as if they were puppets on a string. They left in a hurry, telling me how glad they were that I didn't have a serious illness—except for Jill. She said, "I hope you don't get all deformed and bedridden like my Aunt Alice."

Don't listen to her, I told myself. But her words wouldn't go away. Why me? Why couldn't it happen to someone who didn't like sports? I wanted to yell and scream. It wasn't fair. Was God punishing me for being bad? I'd never hurt anybody, so why did I get a dumb disease like arthritis?

Nine

A few days later Grandpa was closing the suitcase that I was taking to Childrens Hospital.

"Grandpa Al, I forgot my little radio," I said loudly. "Will you pack it for me?"

"There's no need to shout," he said. "I'm not deaf."

I turned to look at him, and he was grinning broadly. "Is that arthritis affecting your eyes, girl?" He pointed to his ear. "What do you think this is, a dadburned earring?"

"Oh, Grandpa, a hearing aid! That's great!"

"Well, when I couldn't hear you call when you were in trouble during the storm, I figured I'd better do something. I just hope I don't pick up radio broadcasts or some fool trucker with a CB."

"Grandpa Al, I love you."

He came over and gave me a gentle hug. "Enough of this gushy stuff," he said gruffly. "Anything more to go in this suitcase? How about the checkers?"

"I don't know if I'll be playing any games." I didn't want to tell him that most kids didn't play checkers. I swallowed a lump in my throat. "Grandpa, I—I'm afraid."

"Sure, you're a little scared. Anything new is scary. I'll let you in on a little secret if you promise never to breathe a word to anybody."

"I promise."

He leaned over and whispered, "My stomach gets all riled up whenever I go to the bank. I'm afraid I'll make some dumb mistake, and the bank teller will think I'm an old fool."

Nobody would ever think that, but it made me feel better to know he felt scared sometimes, too.

"Heather," Mom called from the living room. "It's time to go."

Grandpa locked my suitcase. "I'll take it on down to the car."

Dad helped me down the stairs and into the Warrens' station wagon. Mom had borrowed it so I could lie down during the long trip.

Doug and the Stars all stood there grim-faced. You'd have thought I was going to the hospital for a life-or-death operation. "Hey, guys, I'll be back in a few weeks."

They all tried to smile. My own smile felt pasted on. I'd never been away from home before, except on weekend trips with Grandpa.

"I'll miss all of you," I said, swallowing the lump in my throat. "I'll even miss you, Joey." Dad held him up so he could see me.

As Mom started the engine, Grandpa leaned his head through the open window and whispered, "Remember, you're a Libra. Librans are nine parts steel. No sickness is going to keep you down."

I didn't really think that being born on the twenty-fifth of September was going to make much difference. I nodded, but I kept hearing the doctor say, *There's no cure.*

"Bye, everybody. See you all soon."

* * * * *

The rehabilitation center at Childrens didn't even look like a hospital. I gawked at the large room with its high, domed ceiling of glass. Huge stuffed animals sat on ledges all around the circular room. There was even a merry-go-round. Kids of all ages were eating hamburgers at little tables topped with brightly decorated umbrellas. And everyone was wearing jeans or shorts and T-shirts, not hospital gowns.

Some of the kids looked at me curiously. Some smiled shyly.

A nurse took Mom and me to one of the rooms off the circular room. She was wearing white pants and a pink shirt. The only way I knew she was a nurse was by the nameplate on her shirt.

"Heather, your bed is by the door. Kathy Evans, your roommate, has the bed by the window. We'll bring in a rollaway bed for you tonight, Mrs. Ames."

I looked around. On the wall behind Kathy's bed was a huge poster of the rock group The Wizards.

"Isn't this room wonderful?" Mom said. "How many children are here?" she asked the nurse.

"Usually between 25 and 30."

"Do they all have arthritis?" Mom asked.

"No. We take care of any child who needs therapy."

"Are there any kids my age?" I wanted to know.

"Several. Kathy's 14. She has JRA and is here for some more therapy. She's been coming to us since she was five years old."

"Are you talking about me, Maggie?" a voice said from the doorway.

I turned to see a thin, dark-haired girl. Her brown eyes looked too large for her pale face. She grinned at me. "You must be my new roomie. My name's Katherine. Kathy's okay, but I hate to be called Kate or Kat, and I don't like to get up in the mornings. I hate school and commercials that talk about the minor pain of arthritis. But I love the three R's—rock music, romance stories, and Randolph, my dog."

Right off, I knew I was going to like Kathy. "Hi. I'm Heather. I love the three C's—chocolate, corny movies, and—" I couldn't think of another C word except—"cute guys."

"Have you two had lunch?" the nurse asked us.

"No," Mom said. "We came directly to the hospital."

"Good. We ordered extra trays for you."

"I'm not finished eating," Kathy said. "You can sit with Richard and Sam and me."

I looked at her with admiration. She managed to eat lunch with two guys.

Mom and I followed Kathy. She moved very slowly, head forward, stiff-legged. We stopped at a table near the open kitchen area, and Kathy introduced us to Richard Hobart. He was 15, but he was so short I thought he looked more like 12. Sam turned out to be Samantha Gifford, a girl of 11.

Mom turned to the nurse. "I'm not very hungry," she said. "If you don't mind, I need to buy some clothes for Heather. I thought she'd be wearing a hospital gown."

"Of course, Mrs. Ames. Try to be back by two o'clock. The physical therapist will be seeing how much muscle strength and range of motion Heather has. The therapist will also be discussing the goals for her. We'd like you to be there."

Mom kissed me. "I'll be back in time."

The nurse brought me a hamburger and a glass of milk.

"This place sure isn't much like a hospital," I said. "Do all of you have JRA?" Until a few days ago I'd never even heard of JRA, but I wanted to sound as if I knew all about it.

"Not me," Sam said. "I was in a car wreck."

"I've had JRA since I was a little kid," Kathy said. "And Richard has systemic JRA. He's going to have hip replacements in a couple of weeks."

Richard glowered at her. "Are you going to give her my life history, too?"

Kathy's grin was full of mischief. "No way, Richie. Your life's much too dull."

I had the feeling if anybody but Kathy had said that, Richard would have stalked off. Instead, he just concentrated on his food.

Kathy and Sam asked me about myself. "I live in a little town by the ocean," I told them. "I love to bowl, and I'm a cross-country runner. Someday, I'm even going to run in a marathon."

Richard's head came up, and he gave me a long look. I thought I heard him mumble, "Sure you are."

I avoided his eyes. "At least I hope I can."

Kathy was reaching for the catsup, and for the first time I noticed her misshapen fingers. She saw me staring and held them up. "I didn't get help early enough. They'll never get much better without an operation. But it's no big deal."

"I'm sorry," I said, feeling crummy that I'd been staring at her hands.

"There's nothing to be sorry about." Kathy winked at Sam, then smiled at me. "I'll bet I can whomp you at ping-pong."

"She'll beat the socks off you at swimming, too," Sam said. "I think she's part fish."

Kathy started humming the shark music from *Jaws*.

"Is there really a swimming pool here?" I asked.

"There's everything here," Kathy said. "A pool, a hydrotherapy room, a gym, an activity room for crafts and—"

"Don't forget the school," Sam said with a groan. "We have a couple of hours of classes every day."

I shook my head, amazed at how different this place was from what I'd expected. "I guess a couple of months here won't be so bad after all."

"I've been here a year," Richard said, and slowly got to his feet. He tried to hide the pain on his face, but I knew he was hurting.

When he was out of hearing range, I said, "A year! No way am I staying here a year."

"Some kids stay for only a couple of weeks. It depends on how bad they are."

I sighed with relief. I could handle a few weeks. I looked around at some of the other kids in casts and splints. "I had no idea kids had to have hip replacements."

"Sure," Kathy said. "They replace knees, too. Richard's arthritis is so bad that his joints just cemented. But most kids don't need any operations." She laughed. "I'm waiting until they have head replacements. I never did like this one."

I was glad Kathy was my roommate. In fact, I wished she were one of the Stars. She'd fit right in.

She was wearing a T-shirt that said CAMP WEWILWALK—THIS JOINT'S JUMPIN'. "I like your shirt," I said. "Is that some kind of an Indian name?"

Kathy laughed. "It's 'Camp we will walk'. I've gone there the last couple of years."

"Sounds fun. I've never been to any kind of camp."

"Richard was there."

The way she said his name, I wondered if Richard was special to her.

"He seems so—unhappy," I said.

Kathy gave a little sigh. "He blames all his problems on the arthritis. I wish he'd talk to me, but he just clams up."

I knew how Richard felt. It was hard for me to talk about my feelings, too. But then I thought about Doug and the way we could talk. I decided I'd write to him that night.

* * * * *

When Mom returned with some shorts and T-shirts, I was watching Kathy in the activity room. She was showing a kid how to put on a splint and a cast. The little girl had really knobby knees. It hurt just to watch her move. "I wore these for a long time," Kathy told the girl.

"Did you have a broken leg?" the little girl asked.

"No. The casts were to help straighten out my legs. But they only stayed on for a little while at a time. I wore the splints at night."

Kathy was so patient at explaining things. "You should be a nurse or a therapist," I told her. "You'd be great."

"Who knows? Maybe I will." She sounded surprised, and I wondered if I'd given her an idea to think about.

Richard was showing a little boy how to give a shot to a teddy bear.

Kathy whispered to me, "Andy has to have gold shots every week as part of his arthritis treatment. The little kids don't get so scared when they can stick a needle into a doll or a stuffed animal. It helps if they know what to expect."

Dr. Matthews had mentioned gold therapy for me. I wondered if I'd have to have shots, too.

At two o'clock, Mom and I went in to see the physical therapist. She wanted to see how I walked and how far I could move each joint up to the point of pain. Then she explained to Mom and me why exercise and movement were so important.

I remembered the exercises Dr. Mason had given me. Maybe if I'd done some of them, I wouldn't be so bad now.

"Heather, we want you and your family to understand JRA and learn self-care. If there's anything you want to talk about or ask, please do."

It was all too bewildering, and I was getting tired after the long ride and all the excitement. "Would it be okay if I rested for a little while?"

The therapist nodded. "Actually, you both look pretty weary. I'll have the rollaway brought in so you both can get a nap before dinner."

* * * * *

Mom stayed until after lunch the next day. She was fussing around, making sure I had everything I needed. I could tell she didn't want to go.

She sighed. "I wish we'd known about this place last fall. It's the answer to my prayers."

I hoped she wasn't expecting too much. I kept seeing Kathy's fingers and thinking about Richard having artificial hips.

"Well, I guess I'd better head for home, honey. Joey's probably running your grandfather ragged by now." She gave one more look around my room. "I've stayed in resorts that were worse. I wouldn't mind spending a week here just sleeping."

I remembered how she'd told Dad that she was worn out. A stab of guilt hit me. If it weren't for me . . . . "I'm sorry I've been so much trouble."

Mom gave me a hug. "Don't you even think such a thing. We'll all go away someplace together next year. You just get well."

She picked up her things and started to leave. I panicked. "Mom! Don't go!"

Suddenly the walls seemed to close in on me. I sat frozen, too scared to even cry.

Mom rushed back to the bed and held me close. "Either your dad or I will try to make it over here every week."

"But I can't stay here. Please let me go home. I promise I won't be any trouble. I won't break anything, I promise . . . I promise."

"Oh, honey, broken dishes don't matter. I want you at home, too. But you need the kind of help they can give you here."

"But—but what if I never get any better? Richard's been here a whole year and he—oh, Mom, I don't want to be *crippled*!" I shuddered. "I don't want to be like Jill's aunt. She can't even get out of bed."

Mom stroked my hair. "Sweetheart, the doctor told me that your chances of recovery are good. When Jill's aunt got arthritis, doctors didn't know how to treat it."

I couldn't keep my voice from trembling. "It's just—I feel so—lost." Then it was like a dam bursting. Words tumbled out. "I can't do things with the Stars. They've just been nice to me because I've been sick. And boys won't ever ask me for a date. I'm afraid nothing will ever be the same. What if I can't ever run again? What if I get worse and I'm stuck in a wheelchair the rest of my life, like Doug's dad? Mom, what's going to happen to me?"

She blotted my tears with a tissue. "You've been holding all this inside for too long. Heather, I don't know what's going to happen. But never look back. Maybe you won't be able to do all the things you used to do, but there will be other things just as wonderful."

I wanted to believe her. But it was hard. We sat there for a long time with her just holding me close until the nurse came in to take me for more tests.

"Are you going to be okay?" Mom asked me.

I nodded. "Give Dad and Grandpa and Joey a big kiss from me."

I could feel my throat tighten up. I didn't want to cry. "The nurse said I can call home often."

Mom was blinking her eyes rapidly. "You do what the doctors and nurses tell you and—and—don't forget to brush your teeth." Her voice was all scratchy. She gave me another quick hug and hurried out.

"Tell everybody I'll be home soon," I called. "Tell everybody I"—my voice broke—"love them," I whispered.

Ten

MOST of the time I was too busy to be homesick. I got to talk to everybody at home, and either Mom or Dad came on Sundays. And mail from home really helped.

Dear Stars,
Thanks for the cards and letters. It was so great to hear from you guys.

I started to tell them I'd gotten a letter from Doug, too, but I was afraid they'd think I was bragging.

My fingers don't work too well yet, so I'm writing one letter to all of you.
This place isn't anything like a hospital. You should see the big heated pool. I wish I could heat up the ocean. What a neat pool that would make!

I stopped writing to rest my fingers and

to think of more things to write about.

The pool was for therapy, but it was fun with all the kids yelling and playing games. It was amazing how much easier I could move in the warm water.

I thought about the first time I'd seen Kathy in a bathing suit. I'd wanted to cry for her. I hadn't realized how thin her legs were and what knobby knees she had. But it didn't seem to bother her at all. After a while I hardly noticed the way the kids looked.

I picked up the pencil again.

We work on crafts. My roommate, Kathy, likes to weave, but I'm molding figures in clay. You won't believe this, but I'm pretty good.

I was making little clay animals and crazy figures to give everybody when I got home. Kathy says I should be a sculptor.

Once a week we get to fix the dinner meal. Of course, it's usually so awful that nobody can eat it. I made some of Grandpa Al's famous clam chowder, but it didn't turn out very well. I think it was because I had to use canned clams instead of Rocky Cove clams.

Actually, I ruined it because I let it get stuck to the pan, and it tasted burned.

Be sure to write and tell me all the things you're doing. I really miss you guys.

A lump rose in my throat, and I could hardly see the lines on the pink notepaper. I quickly signed off.

I'll see all of you soon.

Love, Heather

I turned off my light and lay there thinking about home.

* * * * *

Time went really fast. The nurses were always careful that I got enough rest, but it seemed as if every day was full.

It wasn't all work in rehab, though. The exercises we did in the gym were fun. The younger kids thought we were just playing, but I knew the workouts were to make us use our muscles and joints.

Some of the kids who'd had JRA for a long time, like Kathy, used special equipment to help them in the kitchen. But Maggie, my favorite nurse, wanted me to use my hands and arms as much as possible. She would bawl me out for pushing myself up from a chair with my fingers bent into a fist instead of using my open palm. And she didn't want me to pick up heavy things with my fingers, either. I could damage my joints, she said, if I did things the wrong way.

I'd been at the rehab center nearly a month, and I was really making progress. I continued to take the new medicine Dr. Matthews had prescribed, and I was feeling much better. When I didn't hurt so much, the exercises and therapy were lots easier to do.

But Dr. Matthews thought it was wise to also treat me with gold. He didn't think I was improving enough on the other medicine. It would take three to six months to see if the gold therapy would help. But if it worked, he said the results could be dramatic. So after discussing the side effects with my parents, Dr. Matthews started me on gold. Now, every week I have a shot, just like Andy.

July Fourth was a beautiful, warm day. It made me wish I was back on the beach. We had a watermelon seed-spitting contest. I won!

We played other games. Even Richard joined in—until his family showed up. It was the first time I'd seen them. His father was really tall, but Richard's two older brothers were even taller.

"Do you think Richard was adopted?" I whispered to Kathy.

She shook her head. "It's the systemic JRA. He hasn't grown the way he should. I think that's why he's so moody. He'd wanted to be a basketball player like his brothers."

What would I do if I couldn't run again? I wondered. But I was doing lots better. I wasn't ever going to be as bad off as Kathy or Richard . . . was I?

After that, I didn't feel much like playing games. I asked Maggie if I could go in and rest.

As I lay on my bed, I thought about home. I'd been scared to come to the rehab center, but now the thought of going home was even scarier.

Here, the kids didn't stare at you for walking funny. I was afraid the Stars would feel uncomfortable around me. They might not even want to be around me at all.

I picked up the teddy bear that Doug had sent to me. Whenever I felt low, I held it. I couldn't look at it without smiling. It was so cute. It was wearing running shorts, a Rocky Cove T-shirt, and a running bib with the number 1 on it. It even had on a sweatband and running shoes.

The bear made me both happy and sad—happy because Doug had sent it to me and sad because I might never run again.

I got out Doug's last letter and reread it for the hundredth time.

Hi, Heather,

I'm not much good at this letter-writing stuff. Usually, the only time I write is when Mom makes me send thank-you notes at Christmas. But I just wanted you to know we sure miss you around here.

We had to close the alley for a couple of days to refinish the lanes. Mom sends her love.

I closed my eyes for a minute, thinking about Doug. Did he really like me, or did he just feel sorry for the kid next door?

Kathy came in, and I quickly stashed the letter in the box with my other letters from home.

That night, Kathy was quiet. Usually she talked a mile a minute. But we even turned off the TV early.

"Good night, Kath," I said.

"Good night, Heather," she answered, but so faintly I almost didn't hear her.

I had just about dozed off when I heard a soft sniffling sound. Kathy was crying.

"Kathy?" I whispered. "What's wrong? Are you in pain?"

"No, I'm okay," she said in a voice full of tears.

I hobbled across the room and sank down on the edge of her bed. I touched her trembling shoulder. "Is there anything I can do?"

"Not unless you have a tissue I can borrow," she said with a sad little laugh.

I got one from the box on the bedside table and gave it to Kathy. "Just don't return it," I said, trying to make her smile.

"I feel like a jerk," Kathy said. "I—I'm homesick."

"But it's never seemed to bother you before."

"It was the Fourth of July picnic, I guess. Before I got sick, our family always used to go to the lake for a picnic. We'd sit around the fire and sing and tell stories. We'd play a lot of silly games, and the older kids would play softball."

"But you were only five."

"I remember it, though. I couldn't wait until I was old enough to play softball. Now, it seems as if our family never does anything together, and it's all my fault." She sniffled and blew her nose. "I'm sorry for being such a baby."

"Hey, it's not your fault that you got sick. And you have a right to feel sad once in a while, you know. Besides, I've never known anyone who's as cheerful as you are."

"I do okay in the daytime." She gave a long quivering sigh. "But sometimes at night I—I think I'll never get better. Maybe I'll never walk like other kids. Maybe I'll never be able to dance."

"I know how you feel," I said softly. "I have this fear that nothing will ever be the way it used to be. You know?"

"I know. It's like there's a big black cloud over us that will never go away."

I nodded. "But then I see kids worse off than we are, and I'm ashamed."

"Me, too," she said. "But there are times when I almost hate my friends who can run and dance and play softball. Then I feel even more crummy."

"Sometimes, I think maybe I don't want to go home. I miss my family, but I—I'm scared."

I felt her hand touch mine. "Thanks for talking with me, Heather. I didn't know you felt the same way. You always seem so sure of yourself."

"You're kidding," I said in surprise. "Me? I feel as if my stomach's made of jelly. But I thought things didn't bother you. You always seem so happy."

"One of these days my smiling face is going to crack," she said with a little laugh.

We whispered together for a few more

minutes, then Kathy yawned. "If we don't get to sleep, we'll never be able to get up by seven."

I gave her hand a gentle squeeze. "Good night, Smiley."

"Good night, Jellybelly," she said, and lightly squeezed back.

* * * * *

I wanted to show Mom and Dad how well I was doing, but they hadn't been able to visit for a few weeks. Everybody in the family had had the flu. One Sunday, though, Maggie came to the gym to tell me I had visitors.

"Is it okay if I go to my room before they come in?" I asked. "I want to surprise Mom and Dad with how well I'm doing."

"It'll be a surprise, all right," Maggie said.

I went back to my room and stretched out on the bed.

"Right in here, sir," I heard Maggie say.

I looked up, expecting to see Mom and Dad, when Grandpa walked in carrying Joey. "Grandpa! Joey! What are you doing here?"

Grandpa pretended to turn around and leave. "Some fine greeting that is. Come on, Joey, we're not wanted here."

"Grandpa Al, it's great to see you! It's just that I know you hate to drive very far from home."

"I do—so I let Joey drive."

"Are Mom and Dad okay?" I asked.

"Your mother hasn't gotten over the flu as fast as the rest of us did. She's worked herself into a frazzle. She just needs rest."

He gave me a long look. "Aren't you a sight for sore eyes, though."

I patted the bed for them to sit down. "Joey, you've grown a foot."

Grandpa pretended to check Joey for a third foot.

"Oh, Grandpa, I've missed you all so much." I hugged Grandpa so hard it hurt my arms. "I'm so glad to see you. But I'm surprised they let Joey come in."

"They'd better let him in. This little tyke has missed you."

"I'll bet he didn't know I was gone," I said.

"Oh, no? Every day he crawls into your room, and when he doesn't find you, he starts crying. He even calls your name."

"Oh, Grandpa." I giggled. "Babies don't talk at nine months."

"Well, this one does. He says, 'Heh—er, Heh—er.' Show her, Joey."

Joey looked cute in his blue shorts and shirt. How I envied him his blond, curly hair and huge, brown eyes. It wasn't fair that a boy should be so cute—unless he was 14 or 15!

He was grinning at me and making squealing

sounds that did sound a little like *Heh—er*.

Grandpa's face turned serious. "How come you're still in bed? I thought you'd be running the Boston Marathon by now."

"Go to the door and close your eyes," I told him, trying to keep the excitement out of my voice.

He put Joey down beside the bed and crossed to the door. I got to my feet.

"Okay, open your eyes."

I walked toward him, a little flat-footed and stiff-legged, but much better than before.

"I knew you could do it," he said. "Didn't I tell you?"

"You sure did."

"Well, will you look at that!"

I turned around to find Joey taking little stumbling steps toward us.

"Look at that little rascal go," Grandpa said. He picked Joey up and held him in the air.

"Sorry, kiddo, but your sister walks a heap better than you do."

Eleven

JOEY climbed up on my lap. "Grandpa Al, how can Mom get much rest with this little guy around?" I asked.

"That's why I brought him, but your dad and I think you ought to come home now. I just talked to the doc and he says it's okay."

"Now?"

"We need you at home. You'd be a big help keeping an eye on Joey."

My stomach tightened. Home. All those stairs. Joey's toys lying around for me to trip over. People staring. And Mom and Dad . . . would they realize that I still had bad days?

"What's the matter, Heatherbee? Don't you want to come home?"

"Yes—no—I don't know, Grandpa. I want to be with all of you, but . . ."

"I know. I was in the hospital once in World War II. It was nice and safe there. I didn't want to come home to everyday problems."

Grandpa always seemed to know how I felt.

"I'll start packing right now," I said.

"We have to go talk to the doctor before we leave." He gave me a hug. "I'm sorry we have to rush, but my eyesight's not so good at night."

Grandpa helped me pack, then we went to see Dr. Matthews. Maggie and one of my therapists were there. I was really going to miss them.

"You've made extremely good progress while you've been here, Heather," Dr. Matthews said. "It's important that you continue the routine we've established. I see no reason, however, why you can't continue that routine at home."

I nodded. "I promise I'll do everything you've taught me."

"Don't you worry, Doc," Grandpa assured him. "She'll do her exercises or my name is mud."

"Heather, I want to see you in a month to reevaluate you," the doctor went on. "We'll arrange for you to receive your gold injections once a week at my office in North Bay."

I hesitated, not sure I wanted to know the answer to my next question. "Dr. Matthews, do you think I'll ever be able to run again?"

He looked thoughtful for a moment. "I wouldn't recommend it yet. Running puts a lot of pressure on the joints. But you can do all the swimming you want, and gradually increase the amount of walking you do. Then we'll see if your arthritis improves to the point where you can run."

I figured he was letting me down easy.

"I know that you've dreamed of being a marathon runner," he said. "But remember, if things don't work out so you can run, there are a million other opportunities for you. Heather, the whole world's open to you."

I didn't care about the whole world. He hadn't said I couldn't run again, but he sure hadn't sounded very encouraging. I bit my lip and tried not to show my feelings. "I—" I cleared my throat. "I'd like to go tell my friends good-bye before I go."

"Go ahead, Heather. I want to explain a few more things to your grandpa."

I hugged Maggie and thanked her. Then I thanked Dr. Matthews and the therapists, and got out of there before I broke down completely. "See you in a month."

I hurried blindly from the room. *I may never run again.* The thought echoed in my head. I stood in the hall for a minute. I wanted to get myself together before I saw Kathy.

I headed for the hydrotherapy room. I found Kathy in the pool. The smell of chlorine filled the steamy air.

"Kath, I only have a minute. I—I'm going

home today." I told her what had happened. "But I'll be back in a month for a tune-up."

Tears welled up in her eyes, but she was smiling. "I'll probably be gone by then. I'm really going to miss you."

"I'll write—every week. I promise."

"Me, too." She swallowed hard, and I could see her chin tremble.

She stood up in the pool, and we hugged.

Kathy's wet bathing suit was getting me soaked. I was laughing and crying. "So long, Smiley."

"See you, Jellybelly."

* * * * *

When we got home, Grandpa helped me up the back stairs. At the door, I stopped. "Grandpa Al, peek in and see if anyone's in the kitchen. I want to surprise Mom and Dad with how well I can walk."

He opened the door and looked in. "The coast is clear."

"Go in and get them both in the living room. And don't tell them how well I can walk."

He nodded. "I'll yell when they're ready."

I sat on a stool near the archway to the living room. The long trip had made me stiff, but I was too excited to be tired.

In a few minutes, Grandpa called to me.

As I came through the archway, he imitated a trumpet. "Ta da—ta da!"

I walked toward Mom and Dad on the couch. "Look at me, everybody."

Mom started to cry. Dad's Adam's apple was going up and down as if he were going to cry, too.

"Well what's everybody bawling about—" Grandpa began. Then his voice broke, and he stomped off, mumbling, "Dadburned allergies."

Tears were rolling down my cheeks. I'd never felt so good in my whole life.

* * * * *

I was hardly unpacked before Grandpa and Doug started working with me and seeing that I did my exercises. Doug and I swam in the ocean. Sometimes, Dad even went with me.

April was taking ballet, so she'd come over and teach me some of the things she was learning in class. The therapist had said that ballet was a great form of exercise, as long as I avoided the jumps.

The Stars practically killed themselves trying to include me in all their plans. I'd never had so much attention in my whole life. It was nice, but sometimes I felt almost smothered.

August flew by. The only thing the Stars talked about was going to school in Ridgefield.

On the first day at Ridgefield High, I was so nervous I thought I was going to throw up on the bus. If it hadn't been for the Stars, I'd have never made it. I could walk fairly well now, but not for long distances.

My feet and legs were lots stronger, but sometimes my legs felt like a rag doll's.

One day Doug and I finished swimming in the ocean. "Want to walk down the beach to Cave Rock?"

It was one of my favorite spots, and I hadn't been there in months. I sighed. "I'd love to, but it's too far. Dr. Matthews said I should take it slowly."

"Is all this exercise and stuff too much for you?" he asked.

I shook my head. "No. I'm surprised. I get tired, but that's all. It's amazing how much stronger I am. Maybe it's because I've always been into sports."

"You know, I've been thinking," he said. "This year, we're having a 5K walk-for-fun besides the 10K run. Why don't you enter it?"

"A walk-for-fun? Walking over three miles doesn't sound much like fun."

"If you do all the exercises the doctor told you to do, I'll bet you can do it. You just leave everything to Grandpa Al and me. We'll have you running the 10K in no time."

"I think you're both trying to kill me off.

Next, you'll be telling me I should bowl again."

He grinned slyly. "I hadn't thought of it, but it's a great idea."

"I'll check with the doctor," I told Doug.

On my next visit to Dr. Matthews for my gold shot, I asked him if it was okay for me to enter the 5K walk.

Dr. Matthews paused for a minute like he always does when I ask him a question. Then he said, "Well, you've made a lot of improvement over these last weeks. Your arthritis has come under better control. And your muscle strength has improved."

"Does that mean I can do it?" I asked excitedly.

He didn't say anything for a moment. "Heather, it's possible that if you do try to walk too far too soon, it will stir up your arthritis and cause at least a temporary setback."

"But you're not saying no?"

"I can see how important this is to you, and what a boost it would give you."

"I really want to try it."

"And I agree the rewards could be more important to you than a setback that might not even happen."

"Then I can do it?"

He nodded. "But if after three or four kilometers you start to really hurt, just weigh the benefits versus the risks before you go on."

"Oh, thank you, Dr. Matthews, I will. I promise. Thank you." Then I startled him by giving him a hug.

* * * * *

The day before my birthday, the Stars and I were eating a hamburger at Margie's. Doug must have followed us, because he came right in and stopped at our booth. This time he wasn't staring at April. He looked directly at me. "Heather, how'd you like to go to the movie in Ridgefield tomorrow afternoon?"

I nearly choked on my pickle. I couldn't believe he'd asked me right in front of the other Stars. "Uh—well, sure."

"I just got my driver's license. I'll pick you up at one-thirty." And without another word, he left.

As soon as he was out of hearing distance, the Stars squealed and giggled. I was trying to keep cool, but I think my insides were squealing and giggling, too.

"What are you going to wear?" Denise asked. "You can borrow my new pink sweater."

"I'll fix your hair," April said.

"It's just a movie," I said.

"Just a movie!" Ginny cried. "We've been waiting for a year to see who Doug would finally ask for a date." She flopped her head on her arms, pretending to faint. "Just a movie, she says."

"Maybe I should spend my birthday with my family. I mean, Grandpa Al probably has something planned for tomorrow afternoon."

April shrieked. "You're going, and that's that."

So I went.

When Doug came to pick me up, he looked as nervous as I felt. *This is dumb,* I thought. *We've been friends for years. We're just going to the movies, not the senior prom.*

As we were leaving, Mom handed me a letter. "This just came," she said.

I looked at the return address. "It's from Kathy Evans. Remember? She's my friend from the hospital."

"That's nice, honey," Mom said absently. I knew she wasn't thinking about Kathy, she was worried about me riding with Doug. I'd been helping with Joey ever since I got home, and Mom seemed to be feeling much better. But the better she felt, the more she fussed over me.

"You be careful now, Doug," she said. "I'm sure you're a good driver, but there are a lot of crazies out there."

"I'll be careful, Mrs. Ames. I promise."

"And don't let Heather get too tired."

"Mom! Please. I'm going to be sitting."

"I'm sorry. I'm having a hard time not being too protective." She gave a hopeless sigh. "But you two have fun."

As Doug pulled away from the curb, I looked back at Mom. She was frowning. "I guess mothers can't help being that way."

"Yeah," Doug said. "Whenever I get a cold, my mom acts as if I have pneumonia."

On the way to Ridgefield, Doug was quiet. I figured he was concentrating on his driving, so I opened Kathy's letter. It was a birthday card. She wanted me to come to Camp Wewilwalk next year.

I read the rest of her note. "Oh, that's awful!" I said aloud.

"What's the matter?" Doug asked.

"It's Richard Hobart, one of the guys I met at rehab."

Doug shot me a quick look. "You never mentioned meeting any guys at the hospital."

I looked at Doug out of the corner of my eye. He almost sounded jealous. "Richard has to have another operation. He already has artificial hips." I folded the letter. "Until I went to the hospital, I didn't realize just how lucky I am. Doug, it tears your heart out to see some of those little kids."

"They keep coming up with cures. Maybe arthritis will be next."

"I hope so."

I pretended to look at the scenery, but I was really looking at Doug. I wished I knew why he'd asked me to the movie. Was it just because he felt sorry for me?

When we arrived at the movie, Doug had a little trouble parallel parking. His face got all red. It kind of tickled me, though. Doug's so good at everything. It was nice to know he had trouble doing something.

We went inside, and Doug headed for the refreshment counter. We ordered the largest size popcorn and jumbo drinks.

The place was packed, so we had to take seats in the middle of a row down front.

When the show was over and the lights came on, I had trouble getting up. My knees and feet had stiffened. The couple in the two outside seats didn't leave, and it was hard getting past their legs. I stumbled, and Doug caught me.

As I wavered up the aisle, I heard the woman say, "Drunk! And at her age. It's disgusting."

Tears filled my eyes. Doug took my arm and steadied me. "It's okay, Heather."

And it was.

Twelve

BY the middle of October, I felt so good
that I was really tempted to start running
again.

On the day of the 10K, I watched Doug
stretch and bend, getting ready for the run.

He stopped and gave me a long look. "It
must be hard for you seeing everybody getting
ready."

I nodded, glad that he understood.

Gretchen Lundquist came up to us. "Hey, I
heard you're not running this year."

"I may not ever be running again—period,"
I said, trying not to sound bitter.

"Then that fall you took last year really did
some damage?"

"No, I have juvenile arthritis," I told her.

She pointed to the T-shirt Kathy had sent
me. It said FOR MINORS WITH MAJOR
ACHES AND PAINS. "I wondered what the
T-shirt was all about. I'm sorry, Heather. I
liked having you breathing down my neck."

Mom and Dad came over to us, and Doug and Gretchen left to talk to some other runners.

As he took off, Doug whispered to me, "Good luck."

"Break a record," I called to them.

Mom started fussing. "Now, Heather, if you begin to get tired, you just stop—" Mom began.

"Sheila!" Dad said.

"All right, all right. I just don't want her to overdo."

"Mom, I'm fine. I'm in good condition. And these new shoes you bought me are like walking on air." They had been specially made to give me good support.

I looked around for the Stars. "Have you seen Denise and the others?"

Dad and Mom exchanged looks.

"What's going on?" I asked. "Everybody's been acting weird this morning."

"Nothing's going on," Mom said.

"Where's Grandpa Al?" I asked. "He promised to be here."

"That's him coming now," Dad said, and nodded toward the registration booth.

"Where? I don't see—" I stopped. "No wonder I didn't recognize him."

Grandpa was wearing a sweatshirt, sweatpants, and a wide sweatband around his nearly bald head. And he had on mirrored sunglasses. I couldn't help giggling as he came up to us.

"Grandpa Al, you look like a real runner."

"You're darned tootin'," he said, and held up the white paper bib with his number on it.

This year, the run was earlier in the day to correspond with low tide. Usually, by this time I would be nervous and excited, but I couldn't get up much enthusiasm for the walk.

As it grew closer to the starting time, though, the excitement of the crowd got to me. The band was playing, and the red and yellow flags were waving in the stiff breeze from the ocean. Out of habit I did my warm-ups.

"Looks like you're moving pretty well there," Grandpa said.

"I should," I said. "You and Doug have been working the socks off me."

I saw Mom carrying Joey and pushing her way through the crowd. And with her were the Stars. All four of them were dressed in jogging outfits. As they came up to Dad and Grandpa and me, I grinned. "I suppose you guys are going on the walk."

All four held up numbers. "We decided to keep you company," Denise said.

"I knew something was going on. And I think it's great."

"I don't know," April said, looking cute in a pink velour outfit. "I think these new shoes have already given me a blister."

"When's this race going to get going?" Ginny asked.

"It's a run and a walk, not a race," I told her. "Any minute now."

I hardly had the words out of my mouth when the loudspeaker crackled and the run announcer welcomed the crowd. "Because of the large number of entries in the walk-for-fun and the narrowness of the beach this year, we're going to start the 10K run first. The 5K walk starts five minutes later."

The runners headed for the starting line. I waved to Doug.

The announcer gave all the usual safety tips, and the runners took their places. "Good luck, everybody."

The starting line marshal checked to see if the runners had the correct run entry. The announcer called out the seconds. The gun fired, and my heart pounded as adrenaline surged through me. The runners took off, and the ground shook with the pounding of hundreds of feet. But I wasn't one of them.

I turned away so nobody could see my tears of disappointment.

"All right, walkers, your turn next," the announcer called out.

Mom hugged me. "Don't forget what I said. If you get too tired, it's no disgrace to stop."

No, it was no disgrace to stop—not in a walk.

"Just remember," Dad said, "a few months ago you could hardly move."

"I know, Daddy." I guess I should have been proud of all I'd accomplished, but quitting the run last year still hurt. I wanted so much to make up for that.

Grandpa, the Stars, and I headed for the starting line. There were mothers with little kids, older people like Grandpa, and others who just wanted to go for a walk on the beach.

There was no gun, just a crowd of people surging forward. I walked on the outside nearest the water, so I could make my way through the crowd.

"This way," I yelled to Grandpa and the Stars. "Follow me."

At the 2K mark, April and Ginny started to lag behind. "Come on, you two," I called.

"My new shoes are too tight," April said. "I'm turning back."

"Me, too," Ginny said. "We'll meet you at the park." Jill followed April and Ginny.

I had set a fairly brisk pace and was actually passing the other walkers. It felt great to really stretch out my legs in a long stride.

At the 3K mark I turned to see how Grandpa and Denise were doing. They were well behind now. I hadn't realized there were only a few walkers in front of me. If I jogged a little, I could probably come in first. But this was a walk-for-fun. Coming in first wouldn't make up for my not finishing the 10K last year.

I could hardly believe I'd made it this far so easily. And I hadn't even trained for it. Maybe this was my reward for doing everything Dr. Matthews and the therapist had told me, I thought. All the swimming and dancing and exercises that sometimes seemed silly and useless had made me strong.

I looked ahead at the longer 10K course. Being a runner had always been my dream—not dancing or swimming or making little clay figures. But could I do it? Dr. Matthews was afraid I might suffer a setback even finishing the 5K course.

I stopped and waited for Grandpa and Denise to catch up with me.

"How are you doing, Heatherbee?"

"I feel great, Grandpa Al. My knee doesn't hurt. I don't even feel tired yet." I looked again at the rope barrier, then back to Grandpa. "Guess what!" I said excitedly. "I'm going to go on and try to finish the whole 10K course."

He didn't say anything for a minute. Then he pushed up the sleeves of his sweatshirt and said, "If you can make it, I can, too."

"You're crazy, Grandpa Al. You haven't

walked that far in years."

"Easy frazeezy. Remember, I've been working with you." He grinned. "A hot fudge sundae says I can."

"If you make that chocolate cheesecake, you're on," I said. "You'll never get up that hill to the highway."

"Ha! We'll just see about that."

"How about you, Denise?"

"I'll come with you," she said. "At least for a little farther."

We went around the rope barrier. I couldn't see any of the runners ahead. They all must have turned up the hill. "We're so far behind, there won't be any timers along the way."

Grandpa was puffing a bit. "Well, then," he said, "we can pretend we're in the lead. Now, stop talking. I need to save my breath."

I looked over at him. Maybe it wasn't a good idea for him to go so far. After all, he was no kid.

"Are you sure you're okay, Grandpa?"

"Stop yammering and walk."

When we neared the turn going up the steep hill, I was getting tired. We had to walk in deep, soft sand to get to the road. My legs felt weak and trembly, like when you have the flu.

Halfway up, I had to slow down to catch my breath. Last year, I could run up this hill with no trouble, but now my chest was on fire.

I looked back to see how Denise and Grandpa were doing. He was breathing hard. "Grandpa!" I hurried back down to him. "Are you okay?"

He swallowed several times to get his breath. "Don't get all shook up, girl, I just need to sit a spell. You two go on." He gave me a tired smile. "I don't much care for cheesecake, anyhow."

"I'm not going to leave you here," I said.

"I'll stay with him," Denise said. "I need to rest, too."

I looked up at Agony Hill. Now that I'd come this far, I wanted to finish. I wanted to prove I wasn't a quitter. "All right," I said. "But I'll send a medic back just in case you need help."

"You're a worse worrywart than your mother. Now, go!"

I hesitated for a second, then turned back to face the hill. I swear that some giant had tilted it so it was higher than before.

As I climbed, I pretended I was running the marathon. I was in the lead, but the other runners were gaining on me.

As I neared the top, I was gasping for breath. Sweat was pouring down my face, and more than anything, I wanted to drop by the side of the road and rest.

This was the decision point Dr. Matthews

was talking about. But it came later in the walk—at the 8K mark, not at the 4K. I was really tired. I knew I might be pushing too hard, but it was my choice. So what's a little setback? I thought.

I could hear Doug's voice in my ears. *A born cross-country runner never quits until the race is over.*

As I topped the hill, the ambulance pulled up beside me. "We got word from the aid station that there were three runners still out," the medic said. "Do you need help?"

I shook my head. "No," I gasped, "but my grandfather's—back down—the hill."

"We'll check him out." The ambulance moved slowly down the narrow hill.

At the 9K marker, I was so tired, I almost wished I'd climbed into the ambulance. I was beginning to stiffen, especially my knees. I felt like a rusty hinge that needed oiling. Now, I was beginning to think I'd been crazy to even try to go 10 kilometers. But it was still my choice.

I concentrated on moving my legs—right foot, left foot, right, left. And going around and around in my head were the words, *I can do it! I can do it!* No arthritis was going to stop me— not now—not ever!

I heard voices and looked up. Ahead of me, all along the sides of the road, people were standing. I'm dreaming, I thought. I'm so exhausted that I'm hallucinating. People only stand along the way to yell for the lead runners, not somebody coming in an hour after the run has ended.

And then, incredibly, I heard, "Heather! Heather! Heather!"

Now I knew for sure I was dreaming.

As I passed the cheering crowd, it was the weirdest feeling. The cheers and clapping sounded far away. It was like when your ears get plugged and you can't hear very well. I felt as if I were floating a foot above the ground. I could imagine how it must feel to walk on the moon.

But then I thudded back to earth. A heavy weight seemed to have fallen on me. My body felt dead. It was as if I were pushing through a wall of mattresses, not air.

I heard Doug's voice and realized that he was walking alongside of me. "Come on, Heather, it's not far now. You're going to make it."

His words of encouragement helped, and I kept going.

Ahead, I could see the red and yellow flags fluttering at the finish line. A huge crowd was gathered there, all yelling for me. Just a few more yards.

My feet were barely lifting off the ground

now as I made it across the finish line. I raised my arms in the air.

I'd done it! Maybe it was no 10K run, but I'd finished.

Mom and Dad grabbed me. Everybody crowded around. I felt a tug at the hem of my shorts, and I looked down to find Joey jabbering at me. I swear it sounded as if he were saying, Heh–er, Heh–er.

Grandpa hurried over to me. I was glad to see he was okay. He tweaked my nose. "I knew you could do it. Librans are nine parts steel," he reminded me.

I nodded, too exhausted to answer.

The next few wild minutes passed in a blur of excitement. I felt like a celebrity with all the attention. I think I felt happier than if I'd won the 10K. I didn't know if I could ever be a cross-country runner. But I did know that I'd never be a quitter again.

I found out that both Doug and Gretchen had come in first in their divisions.

"Hey, let's celebrate," I said to Doug and the Stars. "Grandpa's buying chocolate cheesecake."

"I have to go to work," Doug said. "I'll come over later."

"I'd love to," Denise said, "but Jill and I are going skating."

"Oh, sure. Have fun." I turned to April and

Ginny. "How about you two?"

"I'm really sorry," Ginny said, "but I have to baby-sit, and April's coming over to show me how to do my hair."

For a second I was hurt, but then I realized things were back to normal. They weren't treating me "different." I was the fifth wheel again.

"Well, Grandpa Al, I guess it's just you and me and Joey. Lead me to that cheesecake."

For More Information

If you would like more information about juvenile arthritis and the services of the Arthritis Foundation, write:

Arthritis Foundation
P.O. Box 19000
Atlanta, Georgia 30326

Ask about family support groups, help in finding local services, and the American Juvenile Arthritis Organization.

You may also want to contact your state's health department to find out about medical services for children with arthritis and other chronic diseases, and your state's education department to find out about educational services for these children.

Arthritis—Some Facts

- Arthritis is a serious condition that causes pain and loss of movement.

- There are three known forms of Juvenile Rheumatoid Arthritis:
  — Systemic JRA ("systemic" means internal organs and other body parts)
  — Polyarticular JRA ("poly" means many and "articular" means joint: many joints)
  — Pauciarticular ("pauci" means few: few joints)

- Arthritis affects nearly 1 out of every 1,000 children.

- Arthritis is usually chronic. This means that it can last on and off for as long as a lifetime.

- The key symptom of JRA is inflammation that causes heat, pain, swelling, and stiffness in the joints.

- Treatment for JRA includes medication, exercise, rest, and joint protection. It is important to begin treatment early. When joint pain or swelling persists, consult a doctor as soon as possible.

- The outlook is optimistic for JRA—it can usually be controlled, and the signs and symptoms may go away. Such a remission may last for months, years, or even forever.

From "A Serious Look at Arthritis" ©1987 Arthritis Foundation.

About the Author

ALIDA YOUNG and her husband live in the high desert of southern California. She gets many of her ideas by talking with people. She's tried to learn to listen—not just to what people say, but to how they say it. When she's doing a book that requires research, she talks to experts. "Everyone is so helpful," she says. "They go out of their way to help."

Mrs. Young developed juvenile rheumatoid arthritis when she was a teenager. But in those days the doctors knew very little about the disease. Instead of therapy, her arm was kept in a cast for weeks. For nearly a year she could only walk with help. "Now," she says, "I hike six or seven miles a day—up hills." She's only able to type with one finger, but her husband says she has the "fastest finger in the West!"

Other books by Alida Young include *Why Am I Too Young?*, *What's Wrong With Daddy?*, and *Megan the Klutz*.